"I DON'T KNOW WHY YOU MARRIED ME ANYWAY!"

"I married you because I felt sorry for you. You were such a lonely little thing, so starved for affection. I thought: why not? I was twenty-eight; it was time I got married. And there was an added bonus—the way you went wild every time I touched you. You looked so quiet and tame, but you could turn into a wildcat. The contrast was fascinating."

"I can see you've had a lot of laughs over it." Her face was crimson with humiliation.

"Oh, no, I never laughed. The loving between us was too good. And now I've found my wife again. I want you back, Sallie."

Linda Howard

An Independent Wife

Silhouette Books

Published by Silhouette Books

America's Publisher of Contemporary Romance

SILHOUETTE BOOKS

ISBN 0-373-48293-0

AN INDEPENDENT WIFE

Copyright © 1982 by Linda Howington

This edition published by arrangement with Harlequin Enterprises B.V.

® and TM are trademarks of Harlequin Enterprises B.V., used under license. Trademarks indicated with ® are registered in the United States Patent and Trademark Office, the Canadian Trade Marks Office and in other countries.

Printed in U.S.A.

Chapter One

The phone on her desk rang but Sallie didn't look up from her typewriter or otherwise indicate that she'd even noticed the noise. With a sigh Brom got to his feet and leaned across his desk to reach the phone and put the receiver to his ear. Sallie typed on, her brow puckered with concentration.

"Sal! It's for you," said Brom dryly, and Sallie looked up with a start to see Brom lying stretched across his desk holding her telephone out to her.

"Oh! I'm sorry, Brom, I didn't hear it ring," she apologized, grinning at him as she took the receiver from his hand. He often ribbed her about being in another world, and it was nothing less than the truth; he often answered her calls as well as his own because usually she was concentrating so hard she didn't hear the phone ring.

He grinned back at her as he regained his seat and said, "It's Greg."

"Sallie," said Sallie into the mouthpiece by way of greeting.

And Greg Downey, the news editor, drawled, "Come see me, kid."

"I'm on my way," she said enthusiastically and hung up the phone.

As she switched off her electric typewriter and reached for the cover, Brom questioned, "Off again, birdie?"

"I hope so," replied Sallie, flipping her long braid back over her shoulder. She loved foreign assignments; they were like bread and butter to her. She thrived on them. Other reporters got jet lag—Sallie got her second wind. Her energy and good humor seemed inexhaustible, and as she rushed off to Greg's office she could already feel the adrenalin flowing through her system, making her heart pump faster and her whole body tingle with anticipation.

Greg looked up as she knocked on his open door and a smile softened his hard face when he saw her. "Did you run?" he asked dryly as he got up and crossed to her, closing the door behind her. "I just hung up the phone."

"Normal speed," said Sallie, laughing at herself with him. Her dark blue eyes sparkled with laughter and dimples peeped out of her cheeks. Greg looked down at her glowing little face and passed a hard arm about her to hug her briefly to him before releasing her.

"Do you have anything for me?" she asked eagerly.

"Nothing for right now," he replied, returning to his chair, and he laughed at the way her face fell.

"Cheer up, I've got good news for you anyway. Have you ever heard of the Olivetti Foundation?"

"No," said Sallie bluntly, then frowned. "Or have I? *Who* Olivetti?"

"It's a European charity organization," Greg began, and Sallie pounced in triumph.

"Oh-ho! I place it now. The world's blue bloods sponsor an enormous charity ball every summer, right?"

"Right," concurred Greg.

"Am I interested?" asked Sallie. "America doesn't have any blue blood, you know, only hot red blood."

"You're interested," Greg drawled. "The shindig is being held this year in Sakarya."

Sallie's face lit up. "Greg! Marina Delchamp?"

"Yeah," he grinned. "How about that, eh? I'm practically giving you a vacation. Interview the dashing wife of the finance minister, attend the ritziest party you've ever imagined, and all on the payroll. What more could you want?"

"Great!" she said enthusiastically. "When is it?"

"End of next month," he grunted, lighting a slim cigar. "That leaves plenty of time for you to buy any new gear if you don't have anything suitable for attending a charity ball.''

"Smarty," she teased, wrinkling her pert little nose at him. "I'll bet you think I don't have anything in my closet except pants. For your information, I own quite a few dresses."

"Then why don't you ever wear them around here?" he demanded.

"Because, boss dear, you have a habit of sending me out to the wilds without a minute's notice, so I've learned to be prepared."

"And you're so afraid that you'll miss an assignment that you keep a packed bag under your desk," he returned, not at all fooled by her retort. "But I really do want you to dress up, Sallie. Sakarya could be an important ally, especially since the oil fields on the northern border are producing so heavily now. It helps that Marina Delchamp is an American and her husband is so influential with the King, but it never hurts to look your best."

"Umm, yes, the State Department will be relieved to know that I'm on their side," she said with perfect sincerity, keeping her face straight with an effort, and Greg shook his fist at her.

"Don't laugh," he warned her. "The boys in Washington are going all out with Sakarya. The King knows the power he has with those oil fields. Through Marina's influence with her husband Sakarya has become more pro-Western, but it's still an iffy thing. This charity ball will be the first time such an event has been held in an Arab country and it's going to be covered by all the news agencies. Television will be there, too, of course. I've even heard that Rhydon Baines will interview the King, but it hasn't been confirmed yet." Greg leaned back in his chair and clasped his hands behind his head. "There's a rumor going around that Baines is quitting television anyway."

Sallie's bright eyes dimmed a fraction. "Really?" she asked. "I never thought Rhy Baines would quit reporting."

Greg narrowed his gaze on her, his attention caught by her tone. "Do you *know* Rhydon Baines?" he asked incredulously. It didn't seem likely. Rhydon Baines was in a class by himself with his hard-hitting documentaries and interviews, and Sallie hadn't been a top-flight reporter for that long, but the girl did get around and she knew a lot of people.

"We grew up together," Sallie said casually. "Well, not really together, he's older than I am, but we come from the same town."

"Then I've got more good news for you," Greg said, leaning back in his chair and eyeing her sharply. "But keep it close. It's not supposed to be general knowledge yet. The magazine has been sold. We've got a new publisher."

Sallie's heart jolted. She wasn't sure if that was good news or not. A turnover at the top could mean a turnover at the lower levels, too, and she loved her job. *World in Review* was a first class publication; she would hate to see it ruined.

"Who's the new head knocker?" she questioned warily.

"Didn't you guess?" He looked surprised. "Rhydon Baines, of course. That's why it's not definite about the interview with the King of Sakarya. I heard that the network offered him anchor man to get him to stay, but he turned them down."

Sallie's eyes became huge. "Rhy!" she repeated in a dazed tone. "My God, I never thought he'd come out of the field. Are you certain? Rhy loved reporting more than—more than anything else," she finished, her heart almost stopping in alarm as she realized what she'd nearly said: Rhy loved reporting more than he loved me! What would Greg have said if she'd blurted that out? She could see her job going down the drain anyway, without anticipating the event.

"The way I understand it," Greg expanded, puffing on his cigar and not noticing the slight hesitation in her speech, "he's signed with the network to do a certain number of documentaries over the next five years, but other than that he's coming out of the field. Maybe he's bored."

"Bored?" Sallie muttered, as if the idea was incomprehensible. "With reporting?"

"He's been on top of the heap for a long time," Greg replied. "And maybe he wants to get married, settle down. God knows he's old enough to have all of his wild oats sowed."

"He's thirty-six," Sallie said, struggling for control. "But the idea of Rhy settling down is ridiculous."

"Frankly, I'm glad he's coming in with us. I look forward to working with him. The man's a genius in his field. I thought you'd be happy with the news, but you look like someone's spoiled your Christmas."

"I—I'm stunned," she admitted. "I never thought I'd see the day. When will the news be made public?"

"Next week. I'll try to see that you're here when he comes in, if you like."

"No, thanks anyway," she refused, smiling ruefully at him. "I'll see him soon enough."

Returning to her desk several minutes later Sallie felt as if she'd been kicked in the gut and, rather than face Brom's questions, she detoured to the ladies' room and collapsed on the sofa. Rhy! Of all the news magazines, why did he have to choose *World in Review?* It would be almost impossible for her to find another job she liked nearly as well. It wasn't that Rhy would fire her, but she knew that she didn't want to work with him. Rhy was out of her life now and she had no room for him; she didn't want to be around him even on a professional basis.

What had Greg said? That perhaps Rhy wanted to marry and settle down? She almost laughed aloud. Rhy was already married—to her, and they'd been separated for seven years, during which time she had seen him only on television. Their marriage had broken up precisely because Rhy *couldn't* settle down.

Breathing deeply, Sallie stood up and smoothed her expression. Worrying about it now would interfere with her work and she was too much of a professional to allow that. Tonight would be plenty of time to plan what she'd do.

That night as she dawdled over the grapefruit half that constituted her supper, her face brightened. The possibility was strong that Rhy wouldn't even recognize her; she'd changed a lot in seven years, lost weight, let her hair grow, even her name was different. And the publisher wouldn't exactly be rubbing shoulders with the reporters; she might go for weeks at a time without even glimpsing him. She was out of the country for long stretches, too.

Besides, would Rhy even care if he discovered that one of his reporters was his estranged wife? Seven years was a long time, and there had been no contact at all between them. The break had been final, absolute. Somehow neither one of them had gotten around to filing for a divorce, but there really hadn't been a need for one. They had gone their separate ways, built separate lives, and it was as if the year they'd been married never existed. The only result of that year was the drastic change in Sallie. Why couldn't she carry on with her job like always, even if Rhy did recognize her?

The more she thought about it, the more it seemed possible. She was good at her job and Rhy wasn't a man to let his private life interfere with work, as she knew better than anyone else. If she did her job and kept out of his way he would never let out any hint of their personal connection. After all, it was all over for Rhy, just as it was for her.

Usually Rhy never entered her thoughts unless she saw him on television, but now that his presence loomed so large in her life again she found the past crowding in on her. She tried to concentrate on other things and managed fairly well until she went to bed that night, when memories of that year swamped her.

Rhy. Sallie stared upward through the darkness at the ceiling, recalling his features and forming them into his face. She could do that easily, for she'd seen him on television any number of times these past seven years. At first she'd been left sick and shaking whenever she glimpsed his face and she would rush to turn the set off, but gradually that reaction had left her, turned into numbness. Her system had protected itself against such intense grief, allowing her to pick up the pieces of her shattered life and try to build again. The numbness had turned into determination and the determination into indifference as she learned to live without Rhy.

Looking back at the timid, insecure girl she had been, Sallie felt as if that girl had been a stranger, someone to be pitied but not really worth wasting any grief over. The wonder wasn't that Rhy had left her, but rather that he'd ever been attracted to her in the first place. No matter how she considered it she just couldn't find any reason why a dynamic man like Rhy

Baines would have wanted to marry a mousy little nonentity like Sarah Jerome. She hadn't been the gay, daredevil Sallie then, but Sarah. Quiet, plump, malleable Sarah.

Unless Rhy had married her just because she was malleable, someone he could control, push into the background when he wanted her out of the way, yet someone who would provide home and hearth when he did wander back home? If so, he'd been sadly disappointed, for she'd been malleable on every point except his job. Sarah wanted her husband at home every night, not flying off to report on wars and revolutions and drug smuggling, the very stuff that was the wine of life to Rhy Baines. She had sulked and nagged and wept, terrified that each time he left her would be the last, that he'd come home in a coffin. She wanted only to hold that strong man to her because she lived only through him.

In the end it had been too much for Rhy and he had walked out after only a year of marriage, and she hadn't heard from him since. She'd known that he wouldn't call her because his last words to her had been, "When you think you're woman enough for me, give me a call!"

Cynical, hurting words. Words that had clearly revealed his contempt of her. Yet those words had changed her life.

Sighing at the sleep that evaded her, Sallie rolled onto her stomach and clutched the pillow into a ball against her chest. Perhaps tonight was a good time to dredge up all the memories and give them an airing. After all, she might shortly be seeing her long-absent husband.

They had been acquainted for years, as far back as Sallie could remember. Rhy's aunt had lived next door to the Jeromes, and as Rhy had been her favorite nephew it was nothing unusual for him to stop by at least once a week when he was growing up. The visits became fewer when he left town, but he never let too long go by without calling in on his aunt. By then he was beginning to make a name for himself as a reporter, and he had been hired by a television station in New York City. Occasionally he would walk across to the white picket fence that separated the two houses and talk to Sallie's father, and if Sallie or her mother were about he would speak to them, sometimes lightly teasing Sallie about growing up so fast.

Shortly after she turned eighteen Sallie's parents were killed in a car crash and she lived alone in the small, tidy house she had inherited. It was paid for and the insurance money was enough to keep her going until she had recovered from her grief enough to begin looking for a job, so she let the days drift by, dreading the time when she would have to go out on her own. She became closer to Aunt Tessie, Rhy's aunt, for each lived alone. Aunt Tessie died in her sleep just two months after the death of Sallie's parents and Rhy returned home for the funeral.

He was twenty-eight, devilishly good-looking, with a dangerous quality about him that took her breath away. He was a man who lived on his nerve and his wits and thoroughly enjoyed it, and he'd just been snapped up by one of the major television networks, working as a foreign correspondent. He saw Sallie at his aunt's funeral and called the next day to ask her out. She had thought then that he must be bored, used to as he was to so much glamour and excitement, but she had known when she looked in the mirror that he wouldn't find any glamour or excitement with her. She was short, pretty enough in a quiet way, but a bit on the plump side. Her short mop of rich, dark hair was a good color, dark sable, but it lacked style and did nothing for her small face with its round cheeks. But Rhy Baines had asked her out and she went, her heart thumping half in fear and half in exhilaration at actually being alone with such a gorgeous, sexy man.

Rhy was a sophisticated adult; he probably meant nothing by the kiss he pressed lightly on her lips when he said good-night after that first date. He didn't even put his arms around her but merely tilted her face up with a finger under her chin. To Sallie, however, it was an explosion of her senses and she had no idea how to control it or mask her response to him. Simply, openly, she had melted against him, her soft mouth fused to his. Long minutes later, when he dragged his head back, he was breathing raggedly and, to her surprise, he asked her out again.

On their third date only his self-control preserved her innocence. Sallie was helpless against her attraction to him, having fallen head over heels in love, yet she was taken by surprise when he abruptly asked her to marry him. She had expected him to take her to bed, not to propose, and she humbly accepted. They were married the next week.

For six glorious days she was in ecstasy. He was a marvelous lover, patient with her inexperience, tender in his passion. He seemed amazed at the fiery passion he could arouse in his quiet little wife and for the first few days of their married life they devoted themselves to lovemaking. Then came that phone call, and before she knew it Rhy was throwing some clothing in his suitcase and rushing out the door with only a hasty kiss for her and a terse "I'll call you, baby," thrown at her over his shoulder.

He was gone for just over two weeks and she discovered by watching the evening news that he was in South America, where a particularly bloody revolution had slaughtered just about everyone in the previous government. Sallie spent the entire time he was gone crying herself to sleep at night and vomiting up her meals whenever she tried to eat. Just the thought of Rhy in danger made her cringe. She had just found him after the nightmare of losing her parents and she adored him. She wouldn't be able to bear it if anything happened to him.

He returned looking brown and fit and Sallie screamed her rage and fear at him. He retaliated and the quarrel that followed kept them from speaking for two days. It was sex that brought them together again, his surging appetite for her wildly responsive little

body and her helpless yielding to him. That became
the pattern of their marriage, with him gone for longer
and longer periods even though she promptly became
pregnant.

They had even quarreled over her pregnancy, with
Rhy bitterly accusing her of becoming pregnant deliberately in an attempt to make him stay at home. She
knew he didn't want children just now and that he had
no intention of changing his job. Sallie hadn't even
attempted to defend herself, for even worse than being accused of becoming pregnant as part of some
scheme was the shameful knowledge that she had been
too ignorant to take precautions. She had simply never
thought of it and she knew that Rhy would be dis-
gusted with her if he knew the truth.

When she was six months pregnant Rhy was
wounded in a border skirmish between two developing African nations and he came home on a stretcher.
She had thought that his close brush with death would
bring him to his senses and for once she hadn't raged
and nagged at him when he returned; she was too
elated at the thought of having him with her permanently. Within a month, however, he was gone on another assignment even though he hadn't fully
recovered from his wound, and he was still gone when
she went into premature labor. The network brought
him home, but by the time he arrived she was already
out of the hospital and their stillborn son had been
buried.

He stayed with her until she was recovered physically from giving birth, but she was grief stricken at losing her baby and bitter with him because he had been absent during the crisis. When he left again the atmosphere between them was still cold and silent. Perhaps she should have realized then how indifferent Rhy had become to her, but it still came as a shock that he could so easily leave her forever, as he did on his next trip home. She had returned from buying groceries and found him sprawled on the sofa in the living room, his suitcase by the door where he had dropped it. His face was drawn with weariness, but his charcoal gray eyes had still held that characteristic bite as he looked her up and down, his manner one of waiting.

Unable to stem the words that jumped to her lips, Sallie began berating him for his inconsiderate behavior, his total lack of feeling for her after the trial she had undergone, the pain she had suffered. If he truly loved her he would get another job, one that would let him stay with her when she needed him so badly. In the middle of this, Rhy got to his feet and picked up his suitcase. As he walked out the door he had said sarcastically, "When you think you're woman enough for me, give me a call."

She hadn't seen him since.

At first she had been devastated. She had cried for days and leapt for the telephone every time it rang. Checks arrived from him every week for her support, but there were never any notes included. It was as if he would do his duty and support her, but had no interest in seeing her or talking to her. She wasn't woman enough for him.

At last, desperately, knowing only that her life wasn't worth living without Rhy, Sallie decided to *make* herself into a woman who was woman enough for Rhy Baines. With feverish determination she enrolled in the local college and set about gaining the knowledge that would transform her into a more sophisticated person. She signed up for language classes and crash courses in every craft she could think of, forcing herself out of her shyness. She got a job, a low-paying job as a clerk at the local newspaper office, but it was her first job and it was a start. With that paycheck every week, her very own paycheck, came something she could hardly recognize at first, but which became larger with each succeeding check: a sense of self-reliance.

She found that she was doing well in her language classes, was, in fact, at the top of her class. She had a natural aptitude for words and languages and she enrolled in a creative writing class. The time that this consumed forced her to give up her courses in crafts, but her interest in writing grew by leaps and bounds and she didn't miss puttering about with paints and straw.

Like a snowball, her forced activities grew in size and scope until she didn't have an idle hour in her day. Once she began making friends she discovered that it was easy, that she liked being with people. Slowly she began to emerge from the shell that had encased her for all of her life.

With all of her activities, Sallie was seldom still and often forgot meals. Pounds melted from her petite frame and she had to replace her entire wardrobe. She went from slightly plump to almost too thin, and as her face slimmed the exotic bone work of her skull was revealed. Without the roundness of her cheeks to balance them her dark blue eyes became huge in her face and underneath them her high, chiseled cheekbones gave her an almost Eastern quality. She had been attractive before, but now she became something more, a young woman who was striking and unusual. Never classically lovely, not Sallie, but now she stood out in a crowd. As her hair grew she simply pulled it back out of her way, not bothering to keep it cut, and the sable-colored mass began to stream down her back in a thick mane.

As she changed physically her entire manner changed. Her self-confidence soared; she became outgoing and found that she had a keen mind and an appreciation of the absurdities of life that made people seek her out. She was enjoying herself, and thoughts of Rhy became fewer and fewer.

They had been separated for almost a year when she realized that as she had grown up, she had also grown away. The weekly check from Rhy was like a revelation, for as she stared at his bold, sprawling signature on the check she was stunned to find that the crippling pain was gone. Not only that, if Rhy came back to her now it would curtail the exciting new life she'd built for herself and she didn't want that. She had made herself over, made herself into a woman who was woman enough for Rhy Baines—and now she found that she didn't need him. She no longer needed to live through him; she had herself.

It was like being released from prison. The knowledge that she was self-sufficient and independent was like a heady wine, making her giddy. Now she understood why Rhy had put his job over her; like him, she had become hooked on excitement, and she wondered how he had lived with her as long as he had.

With a great sense of relief she mailed Rhy's check back to his address at the network, enclosing a note explaining that she had a job and was trying to support herself, therefore his support was no longer needed, though she did appreciate the thought. That was the last communication between them and that had been rather one-sided as Rhy had never replied to her note. The checks had simply ceased to arrive.

Then fate stepped into Sallie's life. A bridge she was driving across collapsed, and though she was far enough across that her car didn't slide into the river below, several behind her weren't so lucky. Without really thinking about what she was doing she helped in the rescue of the people who had survived the plunge into the river and obtained interviews with everyone involved. Afterwards she went to the newspaper office where she worked, typed up a report of the accident, including her own colorful eyewitness description, and gave it to the editor. It was printed, and she was given a new job as a reporter.

Now, at the age of twenty-six, she had completed her degree and was a reporter for one of the better weekly news magazines and her zest for new experiences had not waned. Now she fully understood why danger hadn't kept Rhy from his job, for she enjoyed the danger, the heart-pounding excitement of taking off in a helicopter while ground troops sprayed automatic fire at the aircraft, the exhilaration of coming down in a plane with only one good engine, the satisfaction of a difficult job well-done. She had rented out her house and now lived in a neat two-room apartment in New York, a mere stopping place between assignments. She had no plants and no pets, for who would take care of them while she was halfway around the world? She had no romantic interests, for she was never in one place for long, but she had scores of friends and acquaintances.

No, she reflected sleepily as she finally began to doze off, she didn't want Rhy back in her life now. He would only interfere with the things she enjoyed. But, thinking about it, she didn't think that he would care what she did if by some chance he did recognize her, and that wasn't likely. After all, he hadn't thought about her in seven years. Why should he start now?

Chapter Two

Sallie stood before her mirror and studied the photograph she held in her hand of herself at the age of eighteen. Then she looked back at her reflection and studied the differences. The most obvious change was that now she had cheekbones instead of cheeks. The hair, too, of course, grown from a short mop that barely covered her ears into the thick braid that hung to her waist. The only thing that hadn't changed was her eyes, large, dark blue eyes. However, if she wore dark glasses whenever she thought she might run into Rhy she could continue indefinitely to keep her identity from him.

She had thought about it from all angles and decided not to rely on Rhy's good nature, which was a chancy thing at best. Rhy was hair-triggered, volatile, never predictable. The best thing to do was to avoid him whenever possible and try to keep Greg from introducing her to her own husband as an old friend from his hometown!

Rhy was supposed to arrive that morning; the news had been broken yesterday that the magazine had been sold to Rhydon Baines, who had resigned as a network foreign correspondent and would hereafter devote his time and talents to the publishing of news, except for occasional documentary specials. The entire building had hummed with the news. Veteran reporters had suddenly become uneasy, checking their credits, reviewing their work and comparing it to Rhy's direct, slashing style of reporting. And if Sallie had heard one comment from an excited woman about how handsome Rhydon Baines was she had heard a hundred. Even women who were happily married were thrilled to be working with Rhy. He was more than a top reporter—he was a celebrity.

Sallie was already bored with the entire business. First thing this morning she was going to ask Greg for an assignment, anything to get away until things calmed down. She'd already been three weeks between assignments so no one would think it odd that she was becoming restless. It was more than a month until the charity ball in Sakarya and she didn't think she'd be able to sit still that long.

Suddenly noticing the time, she cast a last quick glance over her slender form, neat and capable in dark blue slacks and a blue silk shirt. Her hair was pulled back and braided into one long fat rope and, as the final touch, she had added a pair of dark glasses. She could tell anyone who asked that she had a headache and the light hurt her eyes; the glasses weren't so dark that she couldn't work with them on if necessary.

Then she had to rush, and as the elevator in her apartment building was notoriously slow in arriving she used the stairs, running down them two at a time and reaching her bus stop just as the bus was closing its doors. She yelled and pounded on the doors and they slid open and the driver grinned at her. "Wondered where you were," he said jokingly. In actual fact, she was a regular bus door pounder.

She made it to the office with a minute to spare and collapsed into her chair, wondering how she had made it across the street without being hit at least six times. The blood was racing through her veins and she grinned. It was time for some action when her usual method of getting to work was beginning to seem exciting!

"Hi," Brom greeted her. "Ready to meet the man?"

"I'm ready to do some traveling," she retorted. "I've been here too long. I'm growing cobwebs. I think I'll beard Greg in his den and see if I can't get some action."

"You're nuts," Brom informed her bluntly. "Greg's quick today. You'd be better off to wait until tomorrow."

"I'll take my chances," Sallie said blithely.

"Don't you always? Hey, why the glasses? Are you trying to hide a black eye?" Brom pounced, his eyes lighting up at the possibility that Sallie had gotten involved in a brawl somewhere.

"Nope." To convince him she raised the glasses to let him see for himself that her eyes were normal, then set them back in place on her nose. "I've got a headache and the light is bothering me."

"Do you have migraines?" Brom asked in concern. "My sister has 'em and the light always bothers her."

"I don't think it's a migraine," she hedged. "It's probably just a nervous reaction to sitting still for so long."

Brom laughed, as she had meant him to, and she made her escape to talk to Greg before Rhy arrived and all chance was lost.

As she neared Greg's open door she heard him on the phone, his voice curt and impatient, and Sallie's eyebrows rose as she listened. Greg was by nature an impatient man, one of the doers of the world, but he wasn't usually unreasonable but his attitude now didn't strike her as being reasonable. Brom was right, Greg was "quicker" than usual, edgy and irascible, and she had no doubt that it was all due to Rhy's impending arrival.

When she heard the phone crash down into the cradle she poked her head around the door and inquired, "Would a cup of coffee help?"

Greg's dark head jerked up at the sound of her voice and his mouth moved into a wry grimace. "I'm swimming in coffee now," he grunted in reply. "Hell's bells, I didn't know there were so many idiots working in this building. I swear if one more fool calls me—"

"Everyone's nervous," she soothed.

"You're not," he pointed out. "Why the glasses? Are you so famous now that you've got to travel incognito?"

"There's a reason for the glasses," Sallie retaliated. "But because you're being nasty I won't tell you."

"Suit yourself," he growled. "Get out of my office."

"I need an assignment," she pointed out. "I'm at the snapping stage myself."

"I thought you wanted to be here to meet your old hometown pal," Greg shot back. "Anyway, I don't have anything to give you right now."

"Come on," she pleaded. "You've got to have a little something. No riots, no natural disasters, no political kidnappings? There's bound to be a story for me somewhere in the world!"

"Maybe tomorrow," he replied. "Don't be in such a hurry. For God's sake, Sal, I may need you around in case the Man gets testy. An old friend is nice to have around—"

"To throw to the lion?" she interrupted dryly.

Abruptly Greg grinned. "Don't worry, doll, he won't tear you to pieces, only maul you around a bit."

"Greg, you're not listening to me," she groaned. "I've been stagnating here for three weeks. I need to earn my keep."

"You don't have any sense," he observed.

"You don't have any sense of mercy," she retorted. "Greg, *please*."

"What's the damned hurry?" he suddenly yelled. "Dammit, Sal, I've got a new publisher coming in and he's not exactly a babe in the woods. I don't expect to have any fun today, so get off my back, will you? Besides, he may *ask* to see you, and I sure as hell want you here if he does."

Sallie collapsed into a chair, groaning aloud as she realized that she would have to tell Greg the truth. That was the only way he would give her an assignment, and perhaps it wouldn't be such a bad thing if Greg knew. At least then he wouldn't keep trying to throw her at Rhy. And realistically Greg had a right to know the circumstances and be aware of the complications that could arise from her very presence.

Gently she said, "Greg, I think you should know that Rhy might not be so glad to see me."

He was instantly alert. "Why not? I thought you were friends."

She sighed. "I can't say if we're friends or not. I haven't seen him in seven years, except on television. And there's something else. I wasn't going to tell you, but you'll need to know. Do you know that I'm married, but that I've been separated from my husband for years?''

Greg nodded, a sudden stillness coming over his features. ''Yes, I know, but you've never said who your husband is. You go by your maiden name, don't you?''

''Yes, I wanted to do everything completely on my own, not capitalize on his name. He's very well-known. As a matter of fact, my husband is... umm... Rhydon Baines.''

Greg swallowed audibly, his eyes growing round. He gulped again. Sallie didn't lie, he knew, she was brutally honest, but—Rhydon Baines? That tough, hard-as-nails man and this fragile little fairy with her laughing eyes? He said roughly, ''My God, Sallie, the man's old enough to be your father!''

Sallie burst into a peal of laughter. ''He is not! He's only ten years older than I am. I'm twenty-six, not eighteen. But I wanted you to know why I want an assignment. The further away I am from Rhy, the better it is. We've been separated for seven years but the fact remains that Rhy is still my husband and personal relationships can get sticky, can't they?''

Greg stared at her in disbelief, yet he believed her. He just couldn't take it in. Sallie? Little Sallie Jerome and that big, hard man? She looked like a kid, dressed all in blue and with that fat braid hanging to her waist. He said softly, ''I'll be damned. What happened?''

She shrugged. ''He got bored with me.''

''Bored with you?'' chided Greg. ''C'mon, doll!''

She laughed again. "I'm nothing like I was then. I was such a cowardly little snit, no wonder Rhy walked out on me. I couldn't stand the separations caused by his job. I made myself sick with worry and nagged him to death, and in the end he walked out. I can't say I blame him. The wonder is that he lasted as long as he did."

Greg shook his head. It was impossible to imagine Sallie as a timid person; he sometimes thought that she hadn't a nerve in her body. She was willing to take on anything, and the more dangerous it was the more she enjoyed it. It wasn't an act, either. Her eyes would sparkle and the color glow in her cheeks whenever the going got difficult.

"Let me get this straight," he muttered. "He doesn't know that you work here?"

"I wouldn't think so," she replied cheerfully. "We haven't been in touch in six years."

"But you're still married. Surely he sends you support checks—" He stopped at the outraged look on her face, and sighed. "Sorry. You refused support, right?"

"After I could support myself, yes. When Rhy left I had to fend for myself and somewhere along the way I acquired a backbone. I like doing for myself."

"You've never asked for a divorce?"

"Well...no," she admitted, her nose wrinkling in puzzlement. "I've never wanted to remarry and I don't suppose he's ever wanted to, either, so we just never got around to a divorce. He probably finds it convenient, having a legal wife who's never around. No ties, but it keeps him safe from other women."

"Would it bother you? Seeing him again?" Greg asked roughly, more disturbed than he cared to admit by the idea of Sallie being married to Rhydon Baines.

"Seeing Rhy? No," she said honestly. "I got over him a long time ago. I had to, to survive. Sometimes it doesn't even seem real, that I was—that I *am*— married to him."

"Will it bother him, seeing you again?" persisted Greg.

"Certainly not emotionally. It has to be over for him, too. After all, he was the one who walked. But Rhy *does* have a temper, you know, and he might not like the idea of his wife working for him, even under a different name. And he might not want me around to cramp his style. I have no intention of interfering in his private life, but he doesn't know that. So you see, it would be a good idea to send me on assignment and keep me away from him, at least at first. I don't want to lose my job." She topped all of this off with a sunny smile and Greg shook his head.

"All right," he muttered. "I'll find something for you. But if he ever notices that you're his wife I know nothing about it."

"About what?" she asked, playing dumb, and he wasn't able to stifle a chuckle.

Sallie knew better than to push her luck with Greg, so she left him with a quick, heartfelt "Thanks!" and went back to her desk. Brom was gone and she was relatively alone, though only a partition separated their little cubicle from the others, and the clatter of typewriters and hum of voices were as plain as if there was nothing between her and the rest of the office.

By the time Brom returned with a steaming cup of coffee she felt more relaxed, her anxiety eased by Greg's promise to help keep her out of Rhy's sight. She finished the article she was writing and felt pleased with the end product; she liked putting words together to form ideas and felt an almost sensuous satisfaction when a sentence turned out as she had planned.

At ten o'clock the buzz of the office ceased momentarily, then resumed at a lower hum and without raising her eyes Sallie knew that Rhy had entered. Cautiously she turned her head away and pretended to search for something in the drawer of her desk. After a moment the buzz resumed its high pitch, which meant that Rhy had left after taking a quick look over the office.

"Oh, God!" a female voice cried over the others. "Just think, a hunk like that is *single!*"

Sallie grinned a little, recognizing the voice as that of Lindsey Wallis, an exuberant office sexpot with more mouth than brains. Still, there was no doubting that Lindsey was serious in her appreciation of Rhy's dynamic good looks. Sallie knew as well as anyone the effect her husband could have on a woman.

Fifteen minutes later her phone rang and she jumped on it, an action that raised Brom's eyebrows.

"Get the hell out of the building," Greg muttered in her ear. "He's on his way to meet everyone. Go home. I'll try to get you out of town tonight."

"Thanks," she said and hung up. Standing, she collected her purse and said, "See ya," to Brom.

"Flying off, little birdie?" he asked, as he always did.

"It looks that way. Greg said to pack." With a wave she left, not wanting to linger, since Rhy was on his way down.

She stepped into the corridor and her heart nearly failed her when the elevator doors slid open and Rhy stepped out, flanked by three men she didn't know and the previous publisher, Mr. Owen. Rather than walk straight toward them she turned and went to the stairs, being careful to keep her eyes lowered and her head slightly averted, but she was still aware that Rhy had stopped and was looking after her. Her pulse thudded in her veins as she darted down the stairs. What a close call!

Waiting at the apartment for Greg to call nearly drove her mad with impatience. She paced the floor for a while; then excess energy drove her to clean the refrigerator out and rearrange her cabinets. That didn't take much time as she hadn't accumulated a lot of either food or utensils. At last she hit on the perfect way to pass the time: she packed her bags. She loved packing, going through her essentials and putting them in their proper place; she had her notebooks and assorted pens and pencils, a tape recorder, a dog-eared dictionary, several paperbacks, a pencil sharpener, a pocket calculator, replacement batteries and a battered flashlight, all of which traveled with her wherever she went.

She had just finished arranging them neatly when the phone rang and she answered it to hear Greg's terse voice giving her the welcome news that he had an assignment for her.

"It's the best I could do, and at least it'll get you out of town," he grunted. "You're on a flight to D.C., in the morning. A senator's wife is making big noises about a general leaking classified information at a drunken party."

"Sounds pretty," Sallie commented.

"I'm sending Chris Meaker with you," Greg continued. "Talk with the senator's wife. You won't be able to even get close to the general. Chris will have a brief on it for you. Meet him at JFK at five-thirty."

Now that she knew her destination Sallie was able to complete her packing. She chose conservative dresses and a tailored pants suit, not her favorite clothes, but she felt that the restrained clothing would help her with the interview, making the senator's wife more trusting.

As usual, she could hardly sleep that night. She was always restless the night before she left on assignment if Greg gave her any warning of it. She preferred having to rush straight from the office to the airport, without having time to think, without wondering if everything would work out, without wondering what would happen if Rhy ever recognized her....

Chris Meaker, the photographer, was waiting for her at the airport the next morning and as she approached him with a grin and a wave he got to his feet, his tall, lanky body unfolding slowly. He gave her a sleepy smile in return and bent down to kiss her on the forehead. "Hi, doll," he said, his quiet, lazily deep voice making her grin grow wider. She liked Chris. Nothing ever upset him; nothing ever hurried him. He was as calm and deep as a sheltered lagoon. He was even peaceful to look at, with his thick sandy hair and dark brown eyes, his brow broad and serene, his mouth firm without being stubborn. And most important of all, he never made a pass at her. He treated her affectionately, like a little sister, and he was protective in his quiet way, but he never made any suggestive statements to her or in any way acted as if he was attracted to her. That was a relief, because Sallie just didn't have the time for romantic ties.

Now he looked her up and down and his level brows rose. "Ye gods, a dress," he said, mild surprise evident in his voice, which meant he was astonished. "What's the occasion?"

Sallie had to grin again. "No occasion, just politics," she assured him. "Did Greg send that envelope he promised me?"

"Got it," he replied. "Have you already checked your luggage?"

"Yes," she nodded. Just then their flight was called over the loudspeaker and they walked over to the boarding area and through the metal detector, then on to the waiting jet.

On the flight to the capital Sallie carefully read the brief Greg had prepared. Considering how little time he'd had, he had included a lot of detail and she became absorbed in the possibilities. This wasn't the type of reporting she usually did but Greg had given her what he had, and she'd return the favor by doing her best.

When they reached Washington and checked into their hotel it looked as if doing her best wouldn't be good enough. While Chris lounged in a chair and leafed through a magazine Sallie called the senator's wife to confirm the appointment Greg had made for an interview that afternoon. She was told that Mrs. Bailey was sorry but she was unable to see any reporters that day. It was a polite, final brush-off, and it made her angry. She had no intention of failing to get the story Greg had sent her after.

It took an hour of phone calls to a chain of contacts but when the hour was up she had interviewed, over the phone, the hostess of the "drunken party" where the general had supposedly revealed the classified material. Everything was vehemently denied, except for the presence of both the general and Mrs. Bailey on the night in question, but when the indignant hostess muttered in passing that "Hell hath no fury" Sallie began to get the idea that Mrs. Bailey was a woman scorned.

It was a possibility. The general was a trim, distinguished man with metallic gray hair and a good-humored twinkle in his eyes. After talking it over with Chris, who agreed with her theory, they decided to pursue that angle.

Forty-eight hours later, tired but satisfied, they caught a plane back to New York. Though her theory hadn't been verified by either of the two principals, the general or Mrs. Bailey, she was content that she knew the reason behind Mrs. Bailey's denouncement of the general. Once they had been checking they had found several restaurants in the capital area where the general had been seen dining with an attractive woman of Mrs. Bailey's general description. Senator Bailey had suddenly canceled a trip overseas to stay with his wife. The general's wife, who had shed twenty pounds and turned her graying hair into a flattering soft blond, was suddenly more in evidence at her husband's side. There was also only Mrs. Bailey's accusation against the general; no one else had added their word to hers and, moreover, the general had not been relieved of his post despite the furor in the press.

Sallie had telephoned all of that in to Greg the night before and he had agreed with her. The article would be placed in that week's issue, and she had barely gotten it in under the deadline.

He was cryptic on the subject of Rhy, commenting only that the man was a mover, and by that she deduced that changes were being made. She would have preferred going on another assignment immediately, but Greg had nothing available and there were always expense sheets to complete and a report to type out. Thankfully, the weekend had arrived and she had a bit more time before she had to go in to the office.

On Monday morning, she reported to work with butterflies in her stomach, but to her relief and surprise the entire day went by without so much as a glimpse of her husband, though the floor buzzed with speculation on the changes he was making in the format of the magazine. She avoided the upper floors, no longer going up to see Greg when an idea came to her; she called him instead, and Brom commented that he'd never seen her stay in one place for so long before.

Tuesday was the same, except that that was the day the magazine hit the newsstands and Greg called to offer his congratulations. "I've just received a call from Rhy," he said gruffly, having picked up the shortened version of Rhy's name from her. "Senator Bailey called him at home this morning."

"Am I being sued?" Sallie questioned.

"No. The senator explained the entire situation and his wife is giving us a retraction of her previous statement concerning the general. You were right on target, doll."

"I thought I was," she agreed cheerily. "Do you have anything else I can do?"

"Just watch your back, doll. Several editors I know are mad as the devil that you're the only one who caught on to what was under everyone's noses."

She laughed and hung up, but the knowledge that her instincts had been right gave her a lift for the rest of the day. Chris came by at lunch and asked if she wanted to share a sandwich with him and she accepted. There was a small cafeteria in the building offering nothing more sophisticated than soup, sandwiches, coffee and cold drinks for those who couldn't get out for lunch, but the meager fare was more than enough for her. She and Chris shared a postage-stamp table and talked shop over cups of strong black coffee.

Just as they were finishing there was a stir among the other people eating lunch and the back of Sallie's neck prickled in warning. "It's the boss," Chris informed her casually. "With his girlfriend."

Sallie sternly resisted the urge to turn around, but out of the corner of her eye she watched the two figures move down the cafeteria line selecting their lunch. "I wonder what they're doing here," she murmured.

"Testing the food, at a guess," Chris replied, turning his head to stare openly at the woman by Rhy's side. "He's checked into everything else. I don't see why he should overlook the food. She looks familiar, Sal. Do you know her?"

Sallie narrowed her eyes in concentration, examining the woman with relief, because that kept her from staring at Rhy. "You're right, she is familiar. Isn't she

Coral Williams, the model?'' She was almost certain of the woman's identity, that classic golden perfection could belong to no one else.

"So it is," Chris grunted.

Rhy turned then, balancing his tray as he moved to a table, and Sallie hastily lowered her eyes, but not before her heart gave a breath-stopping lunge at his appearance. He hadn't changed. He was still lithe and muscular, and his hair was still the same midnight black, his strong-boned face still hard and sardonic, tanned from long exposure to the sun. By contrast the woman at his side was a graceful butterfly, his exact opposite in coloring.

"Let's go," she said in a low tone to Chris, sliding out of her chair. She sensed Rhy's head turning in her direction and she carefully turned her back to him without any show of hurry. Chris followed her out of the cafeteria, but she was burningly conscious of Rhy's gaze on her as she left. That was twice he had stared at her. Did he recognize her? Was her walk familiar to him? Was it her hair? That long braid was distinctive enough in itself, but she didn't want to have her hair cut because he would certainly recognize her then.

She was still shaken when she returned to her desk, due in large part to her reaction to Rhy's appearance. No other man had ever attracted her the way he did and she found to her dismay that the situation was still the same. Rhy had a raw virility, an aura of barely leashed power that set her heart to pounding and forcibly reminded her of the nights she had once spent in his arms. She might be free of him emotionally, but the old physical ties seemed to be as strong as ever and she felt vulnerable.

Out of habit she picked up the phone and called Greg, but he was out to lunch and she dropped the receiver back into the cradle with a ragged sigh. She couldn't just sit there; her nature demanded that she take some sort of action. At last she scribbled a note to Brom asking him to notify Greg that she'd taken ill with a headache and was going home for the rest of the day. Greg would see through the excuse, but Brom wouldn't.

She hated to run away from anything, but she knew that she needed to think about her reaction to Rhy, and once she was home she did exactly that. Was it only because he was her husband, because she knew him as she knew no other man? He was her only lover; she'd never even been attracted to another man as she had been to Rhy. Old habits? She hoped that was it, and when she realized that she hadn't felt the least flicker of jealousy over Coral Williams she was relieved, because that proved she was over Rhy. All she felt for him was the basic urge between a man and a woman who found each other sexually alluring, nothing more. Certainly she was old enough to control those feelings, as the past seven years had proved to her.

The phone rang late that afternoon and when she answered it Greg said curtly, "What happened?"

"Rhy and Coral Williams came into the cafeteria at lunch while Chris and I were there," she explained without hesitation. "I don't think Rhy recognized me, but he kept staring. That's the second time he's stared at me like that, so I thought I'd better clear out." That wasn't exactly the reason, but it was a good excuse and she used it. Why tell Greg that seeing Rhy had upset her?

"You thought right," Greg said, sighing. "He was in my office not long after Brom brought your note up. He wanted to meet you, since you're the only reporter he hasn't met personally. Then he asked me to describe you, and he got a funny look on his face when I did."

"Oh, no," she groaned. "He's latched on to something—he *would!*" she said in swift disgust. "He's as fast as a snake. Did he ask where I'm from?"

"Be prepared, doll. He didn't ask that, but he got your phone number."

"Holy cow," she groaned again. "Thanks for doing what you could, Greg. If Rhy does find out I'll cover our tracks."

Greg hung up and she began pacing the floor, waiting for the phone to ring again. What should she say? Should she try to disguise her voice? But afternoon faded into evening and still the expected call didn't come, so at last she bathed and went to bed. But she slept restlessly, falling into a deep sleep only in the early hours of the morning.

It was the phone that woke her in the morning, the insistent ringing intruding slowly into her consciousness. At first she thought it was the alarm clock and she tried to shut it off but the ringing continued. When she realized it was the phone she grabbed it and in her haste dropped it to the floor. She hauled it up by the cord and at last got the receiver to her ear. "Hello," she muttered sleepily, her voice sounding thick.

"Is this Miss Jerome?" a deep, husky voice asked. There was a husky quality to that voice that tingled her nerves, but she was too sleepy to pick it up.

"Yes, this is she," she acknowledged, stifling a yawn. "Who is this?"

"I'm Rhydon Baines," the voice said and Sallie's eyes popped open. "Did I wake you?"

"Yes, you did," she said baldly, unable to think of any polite assurance to give him, and a deep chuckle made her shiver with reaction. "Is anything wrong, Mr. Baines?"

"No, I just wanted to congratulate you on the job you did in Washington. That was a good piece of reporting. Sometime when you're free come up to my office for a talk. I think you're the only reporter on my staff I haven't met personally and you're one of my best."

"I—I will," she stammered. "Thank you, Mr. Baines."

"Rhy," he corrected. "I prefer to be on first-name basis with the staff. And by the way, I apologize for waking you up, but it's time you were up anyway if you're going to be at work on time.'' With another chuckle he said goodbye and hung up and Sallie gasped as she looked at the clock. She *was* going to be late if she didn't hurry, but Rhy would wait a long time if he was waiting for her to put in an appearance in his office!

Chapter Three

The morning went by without anything happening, though she kept a weather eye out for any sign of Rhy. She had to trust Greg to warn her if she should disappear into the ladies' room, but her phone remained silent. Brom was sent out on an assignment to L.A. and their little cubicle was silent after he left; her nerves began to fray under the strain. She ate an apple at her desk for lunch, not daring to risk going to the cafeteria or even venturing outside the building on the chance she might run into Rhy. She was beginning to feel like a prisoner!

Shortly after lunch Greg called and said, "Come up here, Sal. I don't want to talk over the phone."

Her heart leapt into her throat and she rushed up the stairs to the next floor. Greg's door was open, as usual, and she went in. Greg looked up from the papers he was reading and his expression was grim. "Rhy's secretary just called. He wants your file. I had to send it up. I had no choice. He hasn't returned from lunch yet, so you've got a few minutes of grace. I just thought I'd warn you."

She swallowed the lump in her throat. "Thanks for trying," she said, and managed a whimsical little smile. "It was a dumb idea, anyway, trying to hide from him. He probably won't care one way or the other."

Greg smiled in return, but his eyes were narrowed with worry as she left his office.

Deep in thought and facing the fact that Rhy would know her identity very shortly, she punched the elevator button instead of taking the stairs. She took a deep breath and braced herself.

Abruptly she realized that she was waiting for the elevator and the lights showed that it was coming up. Muttering to herself for her stupidity she turned on her heel and headed for the stairs, but just as she reached them the elevator doors slid open and a voice called, "Sallie Jerome! Wait a minute!"

Her head jerked around and she stared at Rhy for several seconds, frozen in her tracks with horror, then she pulled the heavy door open and took a step, intending to run before she realized the futility of it. Rhy had taken a good look at her and the arrested expression on his face told her that she'd been recognized. She couldn't avoid it any longer; he now knew who she was and he wasn't a man to let the matter drop. She released the door and swung back to face him, her delicate jaw tilting upward pugnaciously. "You wanted to see me?" she challenged.

He moved from his stance in front of the elevator and strode the few short yards that separated them. He looked taut, his skin pulled over his cheekbones, his mouth compressed into a thin line. "Sarah," he whispered savagely, his gray eyes leaping furiously.

"Sallie," she corrected, flipping her braid over her shoulder. "I'm called Sallie now."

His hand shot out and he gripped her wrist, his long fingers wrapping about the fragile bones as if to measure them. "You're not only called Sallie instead of Sarah, you're Jerome again instead of Baines," he hissed, and she shivered with alarm. She knew Rhy's voice in all of his moods, the well-remembered husky quality made it distinctive. It was a voice that could sound whispery and menacing when he was angry, rasping when he was hammering out a point on television, or low and incredibly seductive when he was making love. A wild little frisson ran along her nerves at the tone she could detect in his voice now. Rhy was in a dangerous temper and it paid to be wary of him when he was angry.

"I think you'd better come with me," he murmured, sliding his fingers from her wrist to her elbow and moving her to the elevator. "We've got a lot to say and I don't want to say it in the hallway."

He retained his light but firm hold on her as they waited for the elevator to return to the floor and a copyboy stared at them as he walked down the hall to disappear into one of the offices. "Let go of me," she whispered.

"No way, Mrs. Baines," he refused in a soft tone. The bell sounded as the elevator reached their floor and the doors slid open. He moved forward with her into the box and the doors slid closed, leaving her totally alone with him in that small space. His forefinger jabbed the number for the administrative floor and the elevator lurched into movement.

Sallie summoned all of her poise and gave him a polite little smile, determined to hide the sudden coiling of fear in her stomach. "What do we have to talk about? It's been seven years, after all."

He smiled, too, but his smile wasn't polite; the savagery of it sent shivers down her spine. "Then let's talk about old times," he said between his teeth.

"Can't it wait?"

"No," he said softly. "Now. I've got a lot of questions and I want answers to them."

"I've got work to do—"

"Just shut up," he warned, and she did.

The elevator lurched to a halt and her stomach lurched with it. Rhy's manner made her uneasy and she didn't want to be alone with him, much less go through the inquisition she knew she was in for.

He ushered her out of the elevator and down the corridor to his private office. His secretary looked up and smiled when she saw them, but the words she started to say were halted when Rhy hurled "No interruptions" over his shoulder as he followed Sallie into his office and closed the door firmly behind them.

Sallie stood only a few feet away from him and blinked, trying to adjust herself to the reality of his presence. She had been forced to accept his absence and now she just could not accept his presence. He was a mirage, a figment of her imagination, far too virile and forceful to be real.

But he stood by the door, watching her with those unnerving gray eyes, and he was very real and solid. Rather than meet those eyes she let her gaze drift over his body and she noted automatically the way his dark brown suit fit him impeccably, the trousers molding themselves to the muscled length of his legs. Her pulse began to beat a bit faster and she caught her lower lip with her teeth.

"Rhy..." Her voice quavered and she cleared her throat, then began again. "Rhy, why are you acting like this?"

"What do you mean?" he asked, his eyes glinting dangerously. "You're my wife and I want to know what's going on here. You've obviously been avoiding me. Should I have ignored your presence, as you seem prepared to do with mine? Forgive me if I was slow on the uptake, baby, but I was surprised to see you and you caught me off-balance. I didn't think to pretend that I didn't know you.''

She caught her breath in relief. "Oh, that," she said, sighing, weak now that she knew what he wanted. "Yes, I was avoiding you. I didn't know how you'd take the idea of my working for you and I didn't want to risk losing my job."

"Have you told anyone that we're married?" he barked.

She shook her head. "Everyone knows me as Sallie Jerome. I went back to my maiden name because I didn't want to use the influence of your name."

"That's big of you, Mrs. Baines," he murmured sarcastically, moving to his desk. "Sit down, I won't bite."

She took a chair, more than ready now to answer his questions. If he had been going to fire her he would already have done so; her job was safe and she relaxed visibly.

Rhy didn't sit down but instead leaned against his desk, crossed his long legs at the ankle and folded his arms across his chest. He was silent while his glittering gray eyes looked her over thoroughly from head to foot and Sallie began to tense again. She didn't know why, but he made her feel threatened even when he wasn't moving. Then his silence irritated her and she said tartly, "What did you want to talk about?"

"You've changed, Sarah—Sallie," he corrected himself. "It's a drastic change, and I don't mean just your name. You've grown a mane of hair and you've lost so much weight a good wind would blow you away. And most of all, you're doing a damned good job at something I would've sworn you'd never touch. How did you get to be a reporter?"

"Oh, that was just luck," she said cheerfully. "I was driving on a bridge when it collapsed and I wrote it up and turned it in to the editor of the newspaper and he changed my job from clerk to reporter."

"You make it sound almost logical for you to be one of the top correspondents for a first-class news magazine," he said dryly. "I gather you like your job?"

"Oh, yes!" she said, leaning forward eagerly. Her big eyes sparkled and she tripped over her words in her enthusiasm. "I love it! I never could understand why you were always so anxious to get back to work, but then I was bitten by the same bug. It gets in your blood, hooks you, doesn't it? I suppose I've become an excitement junkie, I only feel half-alive when I'm stuck here in the office."

"Your eyes haven't changed," he muttered almost to himself, his gaze locked on her face. "They're still as dark blue as the sea and so big and deep a man could drown in them. Why did you change your name?" he demanded abruptly.

"I told you, I didn't want to trade on your name," she explained patiently. "I wanted to stand on my own feet for a change and I found that I liked it. As for Sallie, somehow Sarah was changed to Sallie at college and I've been Sallie ever since then."

"College?" he asked, his eyes sharpening.

"Yes, I *finally* got my degree," she said, laughing a little. "After you left I took a lot of courses—languages and creative writing—but when I began reporting it took up so much time that I had to get my degree in fits and spurts."

"Did you go on a diet, too? You've changed everything else in your life, why not get a new figure?" He sounded almost resentful and she stared at him in bewilderment. Surely he didn't mind that she'd lost a little weight? It hadn't even been that much.

"No, I didn't go on a diet, losing weight just happened," she said, her tone reflecting her lack of understanding of the question. "I became so busy that I didn't have time to eat and that still holds true."

"Why? Why did you change yourself so drastically?"

A sudden tingle told her that this was not a casual conversation, a catching-up on old times, but that Rhy had deliberately brought her around to this question. For what reason she didn't know, but she didn't mind telling him the truth. After all, the laugh was on her. She raised her eyes to his. "When you left, Rhy, you told me to call you when I thought I was woman enough for you. I nearly died. I wanted to die. Then I decided to fight for you, to make myself into a woman you'd want, so I took a lot of courses and learned how to do a lot of things, and along the way I also learned how to do without you. End of story."

"Not quite," he said sardonically. "Your rascally husband has reentered and another chapter has started, and to make the plot really interesting he's now your boss. Let's see," he mused, "is there a company policy against employing relatives?"

"If there is," she returned clearly, "I was here first."

"But I'm the boss," he reminded her, a wolfish grin moving across his face. "Don't worry about it, baby. I don't intend to fire you. You're too good a reporter for me to let you go to someone else." He got to his feet and so did she, but he said, "Sit down, I'm not finished." Obediently she resumed her seat and he walked around to take his own chair, leaning back in it as he picked up a file.

Sallie recognized the file as belonging to personnel and she realized that it held her own records. But she had no reason to keep Rhy from reading it, so she watched as he leafed through it.

"I'm curious about your application," he said. "You said no one knows we're married, but what did you put down as your marital status?" he questioned. "Ah, here it is. You've been very honest. You admitted to being married. But your husband's name is, SEPARATED—CONFIDENTIAL INFORMATION."

"I told you no one knew," she replied.

He looked over the application and his brows abruptly snapped together. "Next of kin—none?" he demanded harshly. "What if you'd been hurt, even killed? That does happen, you know! How could I have been notified?"

"I didn't think you'd care," she defended herself. "Actually, I didn't think about it at all, but I can see where you'd want to know. You might want to get married again someday. I'm sorry, that was thoughtless of me."

A vein began throbbing in his temple and she watched it in fascination. It meant that he was furious, as she remembered all too well, but she couldn't think why he should be so angry. After all, she hadn't been killed, so she didn't see anything to worry about.

He closed the file and tossed it back onto his desk, his lips pressed into a grim line. "Get married again!" he suddenly shouted. "Why would I be fool enough to do that? Once was enough!"

"It certainly was," she agreed with heartfelt sincerity.

His eyes narrowed and he seemed to force his temper down. "You don't think you'd like to remarry?" he asked silkily.

"A husband would interfere with my job," she said, and shook her head. "No, I'd rather live by myself."

"You don't have any...er...close friends who object when you take off for days, even weeks, at a time?" he probed.

"I have a lot of friends, yes, but they're mostly in the business themselves so they understand if I go on assignment," she answered calmly and ignored the inference he made. It was none of his business if she had any lovers or not, and suddenly she felt it was important for her pride that he not know he was the only man who had ever made love to her. After all, he certainly hadn't lived the life of a monk, as witness the gorgeous Coral Williams!

"I've read a lot of your articles," he commented, switching to a different tack. "You've been in some tight places—Lebanon, Africa, South America. Don't your *friends* mind that you could get hurt?"

"Like I said, they're in the business themselves. Any of us could come back dead," she returned dryly. "It was the same with you, but you kept going. Why *have* you grounded yourself? You could pick your own assignments, and we heard you were offered the anchor job?"

"Maybe it's a sign of old age, but I got tired of being shot at," he said abruptly. "And I was getting bored, I wanted a change. I'd made some good investments through the years and when *Review* came up for sale I decided to make the change, so I bought it. I'm still signed with the network to do four documentaries for next year and that's always interesting. I have time to do more research, to build a background on my subject."

Sallie looked doubtful. "I think I'd prefer foreign assignments."

He started to say something when the phone on his desk buzzed. In swift irritation he punched the intercom line and snapped, "I said no interruptions!"

Simultaneously the door opened and a soft voice said, "But I knew you wouldn't consider me an interruption, darling. If you have some poor reporter on the carpet I'm sure you've already said all that needs to be said."

Sallie turned her head to stare in amazement at Coral Williams, who was breathtaking in a severe black dress that merely served to flatter her blond perfection. The model was a picture of self-confidence as she smiled at Rhy, fully expecting him to welcome her with open arms.

Rhy said evenly, "I see your problem, Miss Meade," and replaced the receiver. To Coral he said in the same even tone, "It had better be important, Coral, because I've got a lot on my mind."

Such as stumbling over his long-lost wife, Sallie thought to herself, involuntarily smiling as she got to her feet. "If that's all, Mr. Baines . . . ?"

He looked frustrated and ill-tempered. "We'll talk about it later," he snapped, and she took it that she was dismissed. She made her exit with a triumphant grin at a visibly puzzled Coral and gave Rhy's secretary the same grin on her way out.

The first thing she had to do was relieve Greg's mind, so she stopped by his office on her way down. "He knows," she told him matter-of-factly, sticking her head through the door. "It's okay, he didn't fire me."

Greg shoved his fingers roughly through his hair, rumpling the prematurely gray strands into untidy peaks. "You've aged me ten years, doll." He sighed. "I'm glad he knows, that's a weight off me. Is it going to be common knowledge?"

"I wouldn't think so," she hedged. "He didn't mention that. Coral is in his office now, and I don't think he'd want anyone fouling up *that* relationship."

"What a wonderfully understanding wife you are," he mocked, and she stuck her tongue out at him.

With all of the tension behind her she attacked the article she was writing with renewed vigor and finished it that afternoon. Again Chris stopped by her desk, this time to tell her that he was leaving that night for Miami. "Want to see me off?" he invited, and she readily accepted.

Sometimes it was nice to see a familiar face in the crowd when you got on a flight in the middle of the night, so she saw nothing unusual about Chris wanting her company. It wasn't until they were on their way to the airport that Sallie realized that Chris had sought out her company several times lately. She liked Chris, he was a good, steady friend, but she knew that it would never develop into anything more serious on her part. Rather than let the situation stew, she asked him frankly, "Just for the record, why are you asking me to lunch, to see you off, et cetera? Is it for a reason I should know?"

"I'm using you," he admitted just as frankly. "You're good company and you don't expect anything more than friendship. You keep my ego built up, too, because you're a great-looking woman."

She had to chuckle; in her opinion great-looking women were not petite dynamos with more energy than fashion sense. But it was still nice to have a man voice that opinion. "Thanks," she told him cheerfully, "but that still doesn't tell me why."

He raised his sandy eyebrows. "Because of another woman, of course. What else could it be?"

"Anyone I know?" she asked.

"No, she's not in this business. She lives in my apartment building and she's the nesting type. She wants a nine-to-five husband, and I can't see myself settling down into that routine. It's a standoff. She won't back down and neither will I."

"So what will you do?"

"Wait. I'm a patient man. She'll either come around or we won't get together, it's that simple."

"Why should she do all the giving?" Sallie asked indignantly, amazed that even reasonable Chris should expect the woman to make all of the adjustments.

"Because I know I can't," he mocked, smiling a little. "I know my limitations, Sal. I only hope she's stronger than I am and can make some changes."

Then he deftly changed the subject and Sallie realized that he had revealed as much as he was going to. They talked shop for the rest of the time, and she waited with him for his flight to be called, sensing that he felt vulnerable. Leaving for a long trip in the middle of the night with no one to see you off was a lonely experience, and she was willing to give him at least one familiar face to wave goodbye to.

It was after ten when she finally got back to her apartment and she quickly showered and got ready for bed. Just as she turned out the lamp the phone rang and she switched the light back on to answer it.

"Sallie? Where in hell have you been?" Rhy demanded impatiently, and as always his husky voice made her spine tingle.

"At the airport," she found herself answering automatically.

"Meeting someone?" he asked, and his voice became sharper.

"No, seeing someone off." She had recovered her poise, and she quickly asked, "Why are you calling?"

"You left this afternoon before we got anything settled," he snapped.

Mystified, she echoed, "Settled? What's there to settle?"

"Our marriage, for one thing," he retorted sarcastically.

Abruptly she understood and tried to reassure him that she wouldn't cause any trouble in the termination of their marriage. "We shouldn't have any trouble getting a divorce, considering how long we've been separated. And getting a divorce is a good idea. We should have done it sooner. Seven years is a long time. It's obvious that our marriage is over in every respect except legally. I see no reason why it shouldn't be terminated on paper, too."

"You talk too much," he observed, the rasp coming into his voice that warned of his rising temper.

Confused, Sallie fell silent. What had she said to make him angry? Why had he brought up the subject if he didn't want to talk about it?

"I don't want a divorce," he said a moment later. "I've found it very convenient, having a little wife tucked away somewhere."

She laughed and sat up in bed, pushing a pillow behind her back for support. "Yes, I can see where it would come in handy," she dared to tease him. "It keeps the husband-hungry women effectively at bay, doesn't it? Still, we've reached the point where to remain married is foolish. Shall I file or would you rather?"

"Are you being deliberately stupid?" he barked. "I said I don't want a divorce!"

Sallie fell silent again, stunned by his insistence. "But, Rhy!" she finally protested incredulously. "Whyever not?"

"I told you," he said with the manner of one explaining the obvious. "I find it convenient to have a wife."

"You could always lie!"

"Why should I bother? And there's always the chance of a lie being found out. No, thank you for the offer, but I think I'll keep you, regardless of who you have waiting in the wings to take my place."

Abruptly Sallie was angry. Why had he called her at all if he didn't want a divorce, and who was he to make snide remarks about anyone waiting in the wings? "You're just being obnoxious!" she charged furiously. "What's wrong, Rhy? Is Coral crowding you a bit? Do you need your convenient wife for protection? Well, you can hide behind someone else, because I don't need your cooperation for a divorce! You deserted me, and you've been gone for seven years, and any judge in the state will give me a divorce!"

"You think so?" he challenged, laughing aloud. "Try it. I've made a lot of friends and divorcing me could be harder than you think. You'd better have a lot of money and a lot of time before you start, and you'd better have a more reliable job. You're in a rather vulnerable position, aren't you? You can't afford to make your boss angry."

"My boss can go straight to—to hell!" she shouted furiously and slammed the receiver down. The phone began ringing again immediately and she glared at it for a moment, then when it continued its irritating noise she reached over and unplugged it, something she rarely did in case Greg needed to reach her.

Then she turned out the lamp and pounded her pillow into shape, but any chance for sleep was now remote. She lay in the darkness and fumed, wishing she could take her temper out on Rhy's head. Why had he called at all if he didn't want to talk about a divorce? If he wanted to use her to keep Coral at a distance he could just find someone else to do his dirty work for him! Personally, she thought Coral was just his type, someone poised and sophisticated who wouldn't care if her husband was more interested in his job than in his wife.

Then, as if someone had turned on a light in a dark room, she knew why Rhy was so stubborn about not getting a divorce, why he had asked all of those prying, suggestive questions about her friends. If she had learned anything at all about Rhy during the year they had been together it was that he was a possessive man. He didn't want to give up anything that belonged to him, and that included his wife. It obviously didn't bother him that thousands of miles might separate them, that they hadn't seen each other in years, his attitude was that once his wife, always his wife. *He* might not want her anymore, but he was too stubborn to give her up if he thought anyone else might want to marry her. What he didn't realize was that her attitude was much the same as his: once was enough.

She admitted honestly to herself that she would never love another man as she had loved Rhy, and even though she had now recovered from the emotional damage he'd inflicted she didn't think she'd ever be able to love so passionately, so demandingly again. Neither was she willing to settle for a lukewarm, comfortable relationship after having known such a love.

Of course, there'd be no convincing him that she didn't want a divorce in order to marry another man. He'd never understand the need she felt to be free of him. While he'd been only a distant figure it hadn't bothered her, but now that he was going to be around permanently she felt stifled. Rhy's character was too forceful, too possessive, and if he thought he had any legal authority over her he wouldn't hesitate to use it in any way he wanted.

For the first time Sallie seriously faced the possibility that she might have to hunt for another job. She loved her job, she liked working for *World in Review,* but there were other publications. And with Rhy threatening to fire her if she tried to divorce him the best thing she could do was spike that weapon before he had a chance to use it.

Chapter Four

Sallie stared morosely at the keys of her typewriter, trying to force words into a reasonable sentence, but her mind stayed stubbornly blank and so did the white paper rolled into the machine. She had always been so enthusiastic about her work, the words pouring from her in swift, flowing sentences, that this block she was experiencing was tying her nerves into king-size knots. She'd never had this trouble before and she was at a loss. How could she write about something that bored her to tears? And this article *was* boring!

Brom had been summoned to Greg's office and now he returned. "I'm off," he announced, clearing the top of his desk. "Munich."

Sallie swiveled in her chair to face him. "Anything interesting?"

"A Common Market meeting. There's some trouble that could break it up. I'll see you when I get back."

"Yeah, okay," Sallie said, and tried to smile.

Brom paused by her desk and his hand touched her shoulder. "Is anything wrong, Sal? You've been acting under the weather for a couple of weeks now. Have you seen a doctor?"

"It's nothing," she assured him, and he left. When she was alone again she turned back to the typewriter and scowled at it. She hadn't seen a doctor; there was nothing to cure boredom. Why was she being kept in the office? Greg knew that she did her best work in the field, but it had been three weeks since she'd returned from Washington and she hadn't been on a single assignment since then, not even a small one. Instead she'd been flooded with "suggestions" for articles that anyone could have written. She'd done her best, but she'd come up against a stone wall now and suddenly she was angry. If Greg wasn't going to use her she wanted to know why!

In determination she switched off her typewriter and made her way to Greg's office. He wasn't there, so she sat down to wait, and as she waited her temper faded, but her resolve didn't. The natural tenacity that kept her on a lead when she wanted a story also kept her firm in her decision to get to the bottom of why suddenly Greg was ignoring her. They'd always had the best of working relationships, respect mixed with affection, and now it was as if Greg no longer trusted her to do her job.

She had to wait almost forty minutes before Greg returned, and when he opened the door and saw her sitting there, a wary, concerned expression crossed his face before he quickly smoothed it away. "Hi, doll, how's the article going?" he greeted her.

"It isn't. I can't do it."

He sighed at the blunt announcement and sat down behind his desk. After toying with a pencil for a minute he said easily, "We all have problems occasionally. What's wrong with the article? Anything you can put your finger on?"

"It's boring," she said baldly and Greg flinched. "I don't know why you've been throwing all the garbage at me, so I'm asking you, why? I'm good at my job, but you aren't letting me do it. Are you trying to force me to resign? Has Rhy decided that he doesn't want his wife working for him, but he doesn't want to make things look bad by firing me?"

Greg ran his fingers through his gray-brown hair and sighed, his hard, firm-jawed face tense. "You're putting me on the spot," he muttered. "Can't you just let things rest for a while?"

"No!" she exploded, then calmed herself. "I'm sorry. I think I know that it isn't your fault, you've always given me the assignments you thought I could handle. It's Rhy, isn't it?"

"He's taken you off foreign assignments," Greg affirmed.

Though Sallie had braced herself for something like that, to hear the words actually spoken and her suspicions confirmed was a worse blow than she had anticipated. She paled and visibly shrank in her seat. Taken off assignment! It was a deadly blow. All of the passion she'd offered to Rhy had been transferred to her job when he walked out and through the years she'd learned that a satisfying job had enriched her life. She didn't doubt that a psychologist would tell her that her job was merely a substitute for what she really wanted, a man, and perhaps it had been at first. But she was no longer the same person she'd been seven years before; she was a mature, independent adult, and she felt as a musician might if his hands were crippled, as if her life had been blighted.

Through a throat thick with horror she murmured, "Why?"

"I don't know why," Greg replied. "Look, honey, all I know is he took you off foreign assignment. You can still cover anything in the States and several things have come up but I kept you here because anyone could have covered the others and I wanted you available in case something more important developed. Maybe I was wrong. I was trying to do what was best for the magazine, but I know how you are about being in one place for too long. If anything comes up, regardless of what it is, do you want it? Just say the word and it's yours."

"It doesn't matter," she said wearily, and he frowned. Defeat wasn't something he expected from Sallie. Then she looked up and her dark blue eyes were beginning to spark with anger. "On second thought, yes, I do want it. Anything! If you can keep me gone for six months straight, that will be fine, too. The only way I'm going to keep from killing Rhy is if I'm kept away from him. Was this supposed to be kept secret, that I'm off foreign assignment?"

"I wouldn't think so," Greg denied. "I just didn't tell you because I kept hoping I could keep you satisfied on other jobs, but nothing came up. Why?"

"Because I'm going to ask Rhy that same question," she said, and a feline smile curved her mouth at the thought of engaging in battle with her arrogant husband.

Greg leaned back in his chair and studied the suddenly glowing little face, alight with the anticipation of a struggle. For a minute he'd been worried about her, afraid that vibrant energy had been snuffed, but now he grinned in appreciation. Sallie came alive when the going was roughest and that was one of the characteristics that made her one of his best reporters. "Give it all you've got," he said gruffly. "I need you back in the field."

Amanda Meade, Rhy's secretary, smiled at Sallie when she entered. Amanda had also been the secretary of the former publisher and she knew all of the staff; proof of her discretion was that no talk had circulated about Sallie's private interview with Rhy, for which Sallie was grateful. She didn't want any gossip starting about them or Rhy might take it into his head to jettison her entirely in order to halt the talk.

"Hi, Sallie," Amanda greeted her. "Is there anything I can help you with, or do you need to see the boss?"

"The boss, if he's available," Sallie replied.

"He's available for the minute," Amanda confirmed, "but he's got a lunch date with Miss Williams at twelve, so he'll be leaving shortly."

"I won't be long," Sallie promised. "Ask if he'll see me."

Amanda buzzed the inner office on the private line and Sallie listened as she explained the reason for the interruption. After only a few seconds she hung up and smiled again. "Go on in, he's free—and he's been in a very good mood lately, too!"

Sallie had to laugh. "Thanks for the information, but I don't think I'll ask for a raise, anyway!"

Crossing to Rhy's office she entered and firmly closed the door behind her, wanting to make certain that none of their conversation was overheard. Rhy was standing by the huge plate-glass window, staring down at the hordes of people below as they surged up and down the street. He was in his shirt sleeves, with the cuff links removed and lying on his desk and the cuffs rolled back to reveal muscular forearms. When he turned she saw that he'd also removed his tie; he looked more like a reporter than a publisher and he exuded an air of virility that no other man could quite match.

"Hello, baby," he drawled, his rough-velvet voice containing an intimate note that made her pulses leap. "It took you long enough to get here. I was beginning to think you were playing it safe."

What did he mean? Had Greg called to warn Rhy that she was coming? No, she'd just left Greg's office, and in any case he wanted her free to go on assignment. Printer's ink ran in Greg's veins, not blood.

"I don't understand," she said curtly. "What do you mean, it took me long enough?"

"For you to realize you'd been grounded," he replied, smiling as he approached her. Before she had a chance to avoid him he was standing before her, his hard, warm hands clasping her elbows and she quivered at his touch. She tried to move away and his grip tightened, but only enough to hold her. "I was going to tell you the night I called, but you hung up on me," he continued, still smiling. "So I waited for you to come to me."

Sallie was blessed with acute senses and now she wished that they weren't so acute, because she could smell the warm male scent of his body under the quiet after-shave he wore. He was close enough for her to notice that he still, after all these years, didn't wear an undershirt, because she could see the dark curling hairs on his chest through the thin fabric of his shirt. She tore her gaze away from his chest and lifted it higher to his cleanly shaven jaw, to his lips, relaxed and smiling, then higher still, to the direct gaze of those dark gray eyes under level black brows.

With supreme willpower she forced her attention away from his physical attractions and said in a half whisper, "Why? You know how much I love foreign assignments. Why did you take me off?"

"Because I'm not that much of a newsman," he answered dryly, and she stared at him in bewilderment. He released her elbows and slid his hands warmly up her arms, drawing her with him to the desk, where he leaned against its edge and pulled her forward until she stood between his legs. He was more on her level in that position, and the mesmerizing gray eyes looking directly into hers prevented her from protesting at his closeness.

"What do you mean?" she managed, her voice no stronger this time than it had been before. His fingers were massaging the bare skin of her upper arms and involuntarily she began to tremble.

"I mean that I couldn't stand the thought of sending you into potentially dangerous situations," he explained softly. "South America, Africa, the Middle East are all political time bombs and I didn't want to take the chance that you might be caught in one of them if they explode. Europe—even in Europe there are kidnappings, terrorist groups, bombings in air terminals and on the streets. For my own peace of mind I took you off foreign assignment, though Downey nearly had a stroke when I told him. He thinks you're one of the best, baby. I could wring his neck when I think of the situations he's sent you into!"

"Greg's a professional," Sallie defended huskily. "And so am I. I'm not helpless, Rhy. I've taken weapons training and self-defense courses. I can take care of myself. Staying here is driving me crazy! I feel as if I've been put out to pasture!"

He laughed and reached behind her for her braid, pulling it over her shoulder and settling the thick rope over her breast. He began playing with the braid, running his fingers over the smooth twists of hair and the corners of his mouth moved into another smile. "This is quite a mane," he murmured. "I'd like to see it out of this braid and spread across my pillow while I make love to you."

Sallie was rocked on her heels by his words and her cheeks paled. Of all the things he might have said she certainly hadn't expected that! She raised stunned eyes to him and saw his pupils dilated with desire; then he jerked her forward and she lay against him, trapped by the pressure of his powerful legs clasping hers and his arms as they slid around her.

She gasped at the contact of his hard, warm body and, as they always had, her senses began swimming when he touched her. Fighting for control, she turned her head to him to demand that he turn her loose and he took advantage of the opportunity, fitting her more tightly into the curve of his body with the pressure of his arms, and bending his head down. His mouth was hot and forceful and drugging, and she began wriggling in his grasp, trying to escape from her inevitable response to him as much as she was trying to escape from the man himself. By stretching her willpower to its limits she managed to resist the probing of his tongue between her lips, keeping her teeth tightly clenched. After a moment he lifted his head and his breathing was faster, his eyes still eager.

"Open your mouth," he commanded huskily. "You know how I want to kiss you. Let me feel your sweet little tongue against mine again."

He lowered his head again, and this time her will-power wasn't up to the demands she made on it. Her senses exploded with pleasure at the touch of his lips on hers and when his tongue moved demandingly she let her lips and teeth part and he gained possession of the sweet interior of her mouth. With a groan he tightened his arms and in response her hands slid up his arms and shoulders to climb about his neck. Her slim body quivered at the wild storm his kiss was causing, and helplessly she arched against him, gasping her need into his mouth as she realized just how strongly he was aroused.

It had always been like that. From the first kiss they had shared to the last time he'd made love to her, their physical responses to each other had been strong and immediate. She'd never wanted another lover because she'd known instinctively that no other man could arouse her as Rhy did, even now, despite all of the perfectly good reasons she had for not wanting to respond to him. Her body simply did not listen to her mind, and after a few moments she stopped wanting to protest. She felt wildly alive and drowning at the same time, straining against him even as her senses were overwhelmed by the countless pleasure signals her nerves were giving out.

When he lifted his mouth from hers she was so weak and trembly that she had to cling to him for support. Triumph gleamed hotly in his eyes as he held her up with one arm about her waist and with his free hand he cupped her chin and held it still while he pressed swift light kisses across her face and lips.

"Mmm," he groaned deep in his throat, "that still hasn't changed. It's still dynamite."

His words brought a measure of sanity to her fevered brain, and she struggled to put a little space between them. Yes, it *was* still dynamite, and it had nearly blown up in her face! She was a fool if she allowed Rhy to use his physical attractions to make her forget the reason she'd come up here.

"Rhy—don't!" she protested, turning her face away as his lips continued to nibble at her skin. "Let me go. I came up here to talk to you—"

"We've talked," he interrupted huskily, his voice going even lower and rougher, a signal which told her he didn't want to stop. "I'd rather make love now. It's been a long time, but not long enough for me to forget what it was like between us."

"Well, *I've* forgotten," she lied, once again avoiding his kiss. "Stop fooling around! I'm serious about my job and I don't like being grounded because you think that a woman can't take care of herself in a crisis."

He ceased trying to kiss her, but his eyes were impatient as he stared down at her. "All right, we'll talk about the job, then I want the subject dropped. I didn't say that I don't think a woman can take care of herself. I said that I didn't want *you* in a dangerous situation because I didn't think *I* could stand it."

"Why should you care?" Sallie demanded in surprise. "You certainly haven't exhibited much concern for my welfare since you walked out, so don't ruin my job by acting concerned now."

Abruptly he released her and she moved several feet away from him. She was glad of the distance; she needed all of her wits about her in order to handle Rhy, and his closeness clouded her brain with erotic fever. "My decision is final," he informed her curtly. "You're off foreign assignment, permanently."

She stared at him and her stomach lurched sickeningly at his words. Permanently? She could more easily stop eating than she could give up the dangerous excitement of the job she loved! He couldn't have thought of anything that would hurt her more if he'd planned this for years. "Do you hate me so much?" she murmured, her dark blue eyes turning almost to black with pain. "What have I ever done to you to make you treat me like this?"

"Of course I don't hate you," he denied impatiently, thrusting a long-fingered hand through his black hair. "I'm trying to protect you. You're my wife and I don't want you hurt."

"Drivel!" she cried, her small fists clenching at her side. "Being tied down is worse than anything that's likely to happen to me on assignment! I'm only half-alive here. I'm going crazy staring at that blasted typewriter hour after hour with nothing coming in my head to put down on paper! And don't say I'm your wife! The extent of our relationship was that we slept together off and on for about a year, then you went your way and I went mine, and I'm a lot happier now than I ever was with you. You were an even bigger flop as a husband than I was as a wife!" She stopped and drew a trembling breath, trying to control the urge to break something, to hit out at him with her fists. Though she had a temper she wasn't usually so uncontrolled and she knew that frustration had strained her nerves.

"Flop or not, you're my wife and you'll stay my wife," he stated coldly, dropping the words like stones on her head. "And my wife will not go on foreign assignments!"

"Why don't you just shoot me?" she demanded furiously, her voice rising. "That would be more merciful than driving me mad with boredom! Blast you, Rhy, I don't know why you married me anyway!" she concluded in acute frustration.

"I married you because I felt sorry for you," he informed her bluntly, and the simple statement left her gaping at him in outrage.

"You—you felt *sorry* for me?" she cried, and she thought she'd explode with rage. Of all the humiliating things to say to her!

"You were such a lonely little thing," he explained calmly, as if every word didn't lash at her raw nerves. "And so starved for affection, for a human touch. I thought, Why the hell not? I was twenty-eight years old. It was time I got married. And here was an added bonus."

"Yes," she snapped, stalking to the window to stare down at the street below, anything to keep from looking at the mocking dark face, the sardonic eyes. "You got protection from all of your pursuing girlfriends!" With relish she contemplated planting a fist right in his mouth, except that Rhy wouldn't let her get away with that. She knew that he'd retaliate.

He grinned at her temper and walked up behind her, so close that his breath stirred the hair at her temple. "No, baby, the added bonus was the way you went wild whenever I touched you. You looked so quiet and tame, a plump little dove, but in bed you turned into a wildcat. The contrast was fascinating."

"I can see you've had a lot of laughs over it!" she blurted, her face going crimson with humiliation.

"Oh, no, I never laughed," he replied, his voice suddenly becoming soft and whispery. "The loving between us was too good. No other woman ever quite matched you. Everything else about you has changed, but not the way you respond."

Her pride stung, she retorted sharply, "Forget about that. It didn't mean anything."

"I think it did. It means I've found my wife again. I want you back, Sallie," he informed her silkily.

Astonishment spun her around to face him, and she stared up at him with eyes grown huge in her small face. "You're joking!" she accused, her voice shaking. "It's impossible!"

"I don't think it's so impossible," he murmured, catching her close to him and pressing his face into her hair. "I never meant to let you go, anyway," he continued, his voice growing low and seductive. She knew that he was consciously using the erotic power of his voice to disarm and attract her, but recognizing his weapons didn't necessarily give her the strength to fight them. She shivered and tried to pull away, but his grip tightened.

"I thought you'd back down and call me. I was fed up with your nagging and determined to teach you a lesson," he said, raising his head and looking down into her astounded face. "But you didn't call, and I had my career to see to and time got away from me. Seven years is a long time to be separated, but we've both matured in that length of time, and I intend to pull on that leash you still have around your neck, sweetheart!"

"Don't be silly!" she said, shaking her head to deny his casual assumption that she had no choice in the matter, that she would tamely let him lead her about. He had a lot to learn about her! "It wouldn't work out, Rhy. We're two different people now. I'm no longer content to putter around a house. There are so many things I want to do that I may never get around to them all. I have to be on the move."

"I'll be traveling quite a bit with the documentaries I've signed to do. You could always quit your job and travel with me," he pointed out, and she recoiled from that suggestion as if he had thrown a snake at her.

"Give up my job?" she echoed, aghast. "Rhy, are you crazy? I don't want to spend my life tagging after you! This isn't just a job to me, it's *my* career, too. If you want us to be together so badly you quit *your* job." She drew her mouth into a hard line and glared her challenge at him.

"I make more than you do," he drawled. "It would be stupid for me to quit. Besides, I own this magazine."

"The entire idea of us trying to live together is stupid," she blasted him. "Why not just obtain a quiet divorce? You won't have to worry that I'll ask for alimony, I like supporting myself—"

"No," he interrupted, his jaw hardening as temper began to flicker in his eyes. "No divorce, under any circumstances."

"All right, maybe you can make it difficult for me to get a divorce," she acknowledged. "But I don't have to live with you and I don't have to work for you. There are other magazines, newspapers and wire services, and I'm good at my job. I don't need you or your magazine."

"Don't you? Like I've told you before, I have a lot of friends and if I put the word out that I don't want you working, believe me, you won't be reporting. Maybe you could get a job in a restaurant or driving a cab, but that'll be it, and I can stop that too if I want." His eyes narrowed on her and a grin split his dark face. "And in the meantime, you're still my wife, and I intend to treat you as such."

The threat was implicit in his words and she sucked in her breath. Alarm rioted along her nerves as she realized that he intended to resume his marital rights. "I'll get a court order forcing you to stay away from me!" she ground out, too angry now to back down even though she knew that, if dared, Rhy would go to any lengths to get what he wanted.

"A court order might be difficult to obtain if the right pressure is brought to bear," he mocked, enjoying his power over her. "And after a little while you just might decide that you like having me around, you did before. If I remember correctly, and I do, that was the basis of all your complaints, that I was never there. Let's try the whole bit again, hmm?" he murmured cajolingly. "And you wanted kids. We'll have kids, all you want. As a matter of fact, I'm willing to start on that project right now."

Sallie ground her teeth in rage, more upset than he could know by his reference to having children. The beast! "I've had a baby, thank you!" she choked, lashing out in her raging need to hurt him as she'd been hurt, as she still hurt. "And if *I* remember correctly, Mr. Baines, you didn't want him! I carried him alone, and I had him alone and I buried him alone! I don't need you or anything about you!''

''I don't care whether or not you need me,'' he said, his mouth tightening into a grim line at her reckless words. ''I can make you want me, and that's all that matters. You can spit fire at me all you want, but you and I both know that if I want you I can have you. Make up your mind to it, you're mine and I'm not about to let you go. I'm ready to settle down now, for real this time. You're my wife, and I wouldn't mind a couple of kids before we're too old.''

She strangled on the hot words that bubbled in her throat and jerked away from him. ''No,'' she refused savagely. ''No to everything. No to you and no to your kids. Let someone else have the honor! I'm sure Coral would be more than eager to take on the job. And since she's waiting for you now I won't keep you any longer!''

His roar of laughter followed her as she stormed out of his office and Amanda Meade stared at her with round eyes. Without a word Sallie slammed the door and stood in the hallway, shaking with temper. The most galling thing of all was that she was helpless. Rhy had the power to destroy the career she'd so carefully, lovingly created for herself and he'd do it without a moment's thought if he wanted her.

She returned to her desk and sank into her chair, trembling inside. Why was he doing this to her? He couldn't be serious—could he? The memory of his hot kisses returned vividly and blood surged into her cheeks. *That* hadn't changed! Was it just sex that he wanted from her, that and the challenge she now represented to his male ego? She had been his once and she might have guessed that he'd be unable to endure the thought that now she didn't want him.

The only thing was, she wasn't so certain now that she didn't want him. Making love with him was fantastic, and she'd never forgotten the heated magic of his caresses. For just a minute she sank into a delicious daydream of what it would be like to be his wife again, to live with him and sleep beside him and make love with him; then cold reality intruded. If she went back to him, then what? He'd already grounded her. He'd take her away from her job entirely, perhaps even get her pregnant again. Sallie thought longingly of a baby, but she knew Rhy well enough to think beyond that. She could see herself with a child and Rhy growing bored and restless as he had before, resentful that she'd become pregnant. He wouldn't be faithful; he wasn't now, so why should he be later?

He'd tire of her and she'd be both without a job and hampered by a baby. Top jobs in the reporting field were hard to come by and required more than dedication; they required a reporter's whole life. If she left the field she'd have a difficult time returning, carving another niche for herself, and if there was a baby, what would she do then?

The thought of what could happen if she returned to Rhy frightened her and she knew that if she had a

choice she would take her job. It had never let her
down as Rhy had. And she loved what she was doing.
She knew just how precious her independence was,
and she wasn't about to sacrifice it for physical grati-
fication.

She couldn't think what to do. Her nature was to
act, but in this situation there was nothing she *could*
do. Rhy would block any effort she made to get another job unless she disappeared and took another
name, moved to another section of the country. The
thought shook her; it seemed so drastic, but even before her nerves had settled she was making plans. Why
should a little thing like creating another identity stop
her? Hadn't she learned that she could handle almost
anything? She would hate to give up her job, this particular job, but she could find another if she had to.
The important thing was to stay away from Rhy.

It was still a few minutes before lunchtime, but she
jerked the cover over her typewriter and slung her
purse over her shoulder. If she knew Rhy he would
start maneuvering immediately to hem her in, and she
had a lot of things to do to protect herself.

She caught a taxi to the bank where she kept her
checking and savings accounts and closed both of
them out. She didn't know if Rhy could block any
withdrawals if she needed money in a hurry, but it
seemed wise not to take the chance. Over the years she
had managed to save several thousand dollars, enough
that she would be able to support herself while she
looked for another job, and she felt more secure with

the cashier's check in her purse. Rhy would find that she was no longer a helpless little ninny for him to intimidate!

She was rarely hungry, but she'd burned a lot of calories that morning and her stomach was beginning to protest. On impulse she stopped at the bar and grill just around the corner from the *World in Review* building and found an empty booth in a dark corner. It was like going into a cave until her eyes adjusted to the dimness, then she recognized several of the staff either sitting at the bar or tucking into lunch in one of the dark booths. She ordered a grilled cheese sandwich and coffee and was waiting for her food when Chris dropped his lanky form into the seat opposite her. It was the first time she'd seen him since he'd returned from Florida, and she noticed how tanned he looked, even in the dimness of the bar.

"Florida suits you," she commented. "How have you been?"

He shrugged, his quiet face wry. "I'm still at a standoff, if that's what you're asking. What about you, doll? I've heard a rumor that you've been grounded."

"It's true," Sallie admitted, frowning. "Orders from the top."

"Baines himself? What'd you do?"

"It's not what I did, it's what I am. He thinks foreign assignment is too dangerous for me."

Chris snorted in disbelief. "C'mon, Baines is too good a newsman to ground you for a stupid reason like that. Level with me, Sal. What's going on? I saw him staring at you that day in the cafeteria."

"Oh, it's true that he thinks foreign assignment is too dangerous for me," she insisted. "But that's only part of the reason. He thinks I'd be a nice addition to his personal scalp collection, if you get my meaning. Unfortunately, I don't agree."

Chris whistled soundlessly through his teeth. "Big boss is after you, eh? Well, I agree with him that you're a fetching little witch. The only difference is, I never had the guts to tackle you."

Sallie exploded into laughter, knowing that while Chris might like her well enough he'd never been attracted to her romantically. Though he was the footloose type he was attracted to nesting women; he wanted someone who could provide a stable base for him when he returned from his wanderings. Sallie was too much of a wanderer herself for Chris to be interested. He kept a straight face while she rocked with laughter, holding her sides, but his brown eyes danced with amusement.

Afterward they returned to work together, and as they entered the lobby Chris had his arm affectionately around her waist. The first person Sallie saw was Rhy, waiting for the elevator, and as he looked at them and saw Chris with his arm about her his eyes flared, then narrowed to furious slits.

"Uh-oh, trouble," Chris muttered to her, then gave her a grin. As the elevator opened and Rhy stepped in

Chris compounded his sins by hugging her close and kissing the top of her head. In the last glimpse Sallie had of Rhy before the doors closed and hid him from view he looked murderous.

Chapter Five

"You fool," Sallie whispered to Chris, torn between laughter and genuine concern. Rhy was a dangerous man when he was angry. He was strong enough and wild enough and mean enough to handle just about anyone he wanted to handle, and he'd taken a lot of specialized training. Underneath his perfectly tailored three-piece suits Rhy was a half-civilized commando and he could hurt Chris badly. "Are you trying to get yourself killed? Rhy has a hair-trigger temper!"

"I didn't want him to take you for granted," Chris explained lazily. He gave her a crooked grin. "Feel free to use me any time you need the safety of numbers, the least I can do is return the favors you've done me. I use you, you use me in return.''

Sallie drew in her breath. The idea was tempting, to pretend to Rhy that she was wildly in love with Chris, except that she didn't think she could act well enough to make it convincing and she would hate to push Rhy far enough that he lost his temper and hurt Chris.

"Thanks for the offer, but I don't think it'd be very smart to act out our charades in front of him," she declined. "I like your face as it is. But if you don't mind I'll throw up your name as a smoke screen to hide behind."

"Okay by me." He regarded her seriously. "Why are you trying to get away from him? He's got everything a man—or a woman—could want."

"I knew Rhy before he bought the magazine," Sallie explained with caution, not wanting to tell him too much. "He wants to renew the relationship and I don't. It's that simple."

"Except for the feeling that you're leaving a lot untold, I believe you," Chris mused almost to himself and left her with a smile.

After returning to her desk Sallie waited all afternoon for a call summoning her to Rhy's office, but the call didn't materialize and she finally realized that he was more subtle than that. He'd let her worry about it, become anxious and vulnerable. She'd show him!

With a flourish she pushed aside the article she'd been working on and rolled a clean sheet of paper into the typewriter. If Rhy wanted to play dirty, then she had no scruples about not doing her work. Instead of concentrating on that stupid article she'd begin her memoirs! If she wrote her life story down as it happened, when she got old it would be finished and she wouldn't have to try to remember all of the details!

Adrenalin flowed through her veins and her fingers flew over the typewriter keys. For the first time in weeks words spilled out of her brain and she scarcely paused to get them in order. She felt elated, alive again. Enthusiasm pulsed through her body.

Suddenly she dropped her hands, staring at what she'd written. Why play around with her memoirs? Why not take her own experiences and weave them into a novel? She'd always wanted to write a book but she'd never had the time. Now she had the time, and she wanted to laugh aloud at the thought of using Rhy's time and money to begin a new career for herself.

Feverishly she put a fresh page in the typewriter, then sat for several minutes, stumped by her first problem—what name should she use for her heroine? Could she just leave a blank space and insert the name later? Then she realized that she had to have a name before she could visualize her character, and that thought led her to ponder the physical attributes of her creation. Writing a book was different from writing an article of an eyewitness report. Then she had facts to deal with, but with fiction she had to create the details herself. Except for that first creative writing course she was trained in facts and this was harder than she'd imagined.

But before the day was over she had sweated eight pages out of her imagination and she glared impatiently at the clock, which insisted that it was time she left. She slid her precious eight pages into a folder and tucked it under her arm. She would work on them at home, on her own typewriter.

Seldom had anything held her concentration in such a tight grip and when she finally went to bed that night the plot and scenes kept darting around in her mind. This was a challenge that equaled the most dangerous of assignments, and she felt the same enthusiasm, the same drive to get it accomplished. She almost resented the hours she was forced to waste sleeping, but at last she drifted off into a deep, dreamless sleep, the most restful she'd had in weeks.

For a week she worked on the manuscript during every spare moment, taking it to work with her, sitting up late at night and typing until she was so tired that she had to sleep. Rhy didn't call her and she was so caught up in her project that she ceased waiting for him to make a move. She was aware of his silence only with the outer edge of her consciousness, and she didn't worry about it. So long as he didn't try to resume their relationship she was content to let time slide by and, judging by the number of times she saw Coral Williams either entering or leaving the building, Rhy felt no sense of urgency either.

She was ready to leave one afternoon when her phone rang, which startled her, as that had become a rarity. Since Brom was still away she snatched it up and heard Rhy's gravelly voice say tersely, "Get up here, Sallie. We have a problem."

Staring at the phone after he'd hung up, Sallie wondered about the nature of the "problem." Did he mean that they personally had a problem—if so, she had to agree—or did he mean that the magazine had a problem? Had something come up that required her personal qualifications? Was Rhy backed into a corner where he would have to use her or lose a story? She relished that thought as she made her way up to Rhy's office, wondering just how he would handle that situation.

Amanda waved her into Rhy's office with an urgent "They're waiting for you!" and when she entered she saw that Greg was also present, prowling restlessly about the office while Rhy was sprawled back in his big chair with his feet propped on his desk; he looked physically relaxed, but the glitter of his eyes revealed his mental alertness.

Greg turned as she entered and glared at her, his jaw belligerent. He always looked like that when he was upset and Sallie caught her breath in alarm.

Without greeting Rhy she said huskily to Greg, "What's wrong? Has anyone been hurt?" Two years ago one of her closest friends had been killed in South America while covering a revolution, and the tragedy had made her highly sensitive to the risks they all took.

She never worried about herself, but now she braced herself to receive the news that another reporter had been wounded, perhaps killed. Her tension was evident in her low-toned voice and Greg picked it up immediately.

"No, no one's been hurt," he assured her gently, remembering the only time he'd ever seen her break down, when he had told her that Artie Hendricks had been killed.

She sighed in relief and sank into a chair, glancing at Rhy to find his face still, his eyes furious.

Puzzled, she looked back at Greg. "Then what's wrong?"

"The Sakaryan charity ball is next week," Greg informed her, crossing the office to sit down beside her.

"Yes, I know. I was supposed to cover it," she said dryly and shot a scathing look at Rhy. "Who're you sending in my place?"

"I *was* sending Andy Wallace and Patricia King," Greg snapped. "But Marina Delchamp has refused to grant a personal interview. Dammit!" he exploded in frustration, pounding his fist on the arm of the chair. "It was all set up and now she refuses!"

"That doesn't sound like Marina," Sallie protested. "She's not at all snobbish. There must be a reason."

"There is," Rhy drawled the answer from his relaxed position. "She won't talk to anyone but you, or so she says. Why does it have to be you? Do you know her personally?"

Sallie grinned as she realized that her wishful thinking had come true—Marina had placed Rhy between a rock and a hard place, and he wasn't enjoying the situation.

"Yes, she's a friend of mine," she admitted, and if Rhy thought it strange that she knew the gorgeous ex-model he said nothing. Now Marina was the wife of one of the most powerful men in Sakarya and in charge of the charity ball, and she could choose any reporter she wanted.

"Talk to her, convince her to talk to Patricia King instead of you," Rhy ordered. "Or get the interview over the phone." The satisfaction in his tone revealed that he thought he'd just solved the entire problem and she bristled, but struggled to hide her temper.

"I suppose when you're the wife of the finance minister you can give interviews or not, whichever you want," she said casually.

"Sallie," Rhy informed her with deadly calm, "I'm ordering you to get that interview over the phone."

"But it won't work!" she said, widening her eyes in innocence. "Marina can talk to me whenever she'd like if that's all she wants. She wants to *see* me. And I have an invitation to the ball anyway," she finished smugly. She had been intending to take on part of her vacation next week and fly to Sakarya at her own expense, but now she saw a way of defeating Rhy and it was all she could do to stop herself from laughing aloud.

"It won't work," Rhy warned softly. "I said no foreign assignments and I meant it. You can't go."

Beside her, Greg cursed beneath his breath in frustration and got to his feet, shoving his fists into his pockets. "She's the best reporter I've got!" he said in restrained violence. "You're wasting her!"

"I'm not wasting her," Rhy snarled, coming out of his chair with a lithe twist of his body that had him instantly poised, ready to react. In that instant Sallie read danger in his narrowed eyes. "I've told you before, Downey, she's off anything that even smells like it might be dangerous, and that includes any damned party in an oil-rich desert where every power in the world is jockeying around trying to figure out how to get control of that oil!"

"Are you blind?" Greg bellowed. "She thrives on danger. She carries it around with her! Dammit, man, she can't even catch a bus in a normal manner! Her everyday life would turn a sane person's hair gray!"

Deftly Sallie put herself between the two big, angry men and tilted her delicate jaw at Rhy. "If Marina refuses to see Patricia I suppose you just won't get an interview," she said, bringing the conversation back to its original subject. Triumph gleamed in her dark blue eyes. "It's me or no one. How much of a newsman are you?"

His jaw clenched in anger, but he shot a look at Greg. "Get out of here," he ordered harshly, jerking his eyes back to her. "My answer is still no."

"Suit yourself." She left the office with more poise than she would have thought possible, but chuckled to herself as she collected her belongings and left the building.

She wasn't surprised the next morning when she was directed to Rhy's office as soon as she entered the building. She stalled for a few moments, enjoying making him wait while she put up her shoulder bag and locked the manuscript in her desk, then she carefully wiped all traces of amusement from her expression as she went to meet him.

Instead of the frustrated anger she'd expected to see on his face he wore a look of intense satisfaction, and she felt a twinge of uneasiness. "I've solved our problem," he almost purred, moving close to her and reaching out to stroke her hair.

Diverted, she slapped his hand away in irritation. "I'm going to cut my hair!" she said curtly. "Maybe then you'll keep your hands to yourself."

"Don't cut it," he advised. "You wouldn't like the consequences."

"I'll cut my hair if I feel like it. It's nothing to you!"

"We won't argue that now, but I'm warning you, don't cut your hair or I'll turn you over my knee." With that threat he left the subject and quirked an inquiring eyebrow at her. "Don't you want to hear about my solution?"

"No. If you like it that well I know I'll hate it," she said, admitting fantastically that he'd obviously thought of some way to get around Marina.

"I wouldn't say that," he murmured. "You used to like it quite well. You can go to Sakarya, darling." He paused and watched her eyes light up with delight, then he delivered the bomb. "And I'm going with you."

Aghast, Sallie stared up at him. Her thoughts whirled madly as she tried to think of some way out of this situation, but all she could say was, "You can't do that," in weak protest.

"Of course I can," he said, smiling in a predatory manner that gave her chills. "I own this magazine and I'm a newsman. Other than that, I'm your husband—all excellent reasons why I can go to Sakarya with you."

"But I don't want you along! I don't need you."

"Poor baby," he said in mock sympathy, then reverted to his normal tone. "There's no way out of it. If you go, I go. I want to make certain that silky skin of yours stays whole."

"I'm not a child or an idiot. I can take care of myself."

"So you say, but you still aren't changing my mind. Sorry if I've messed up your plans. Did you have it set for your boyfriend to go along with you? What's his name—the photographer?"

The skin on the back of her neck prickled as she caught the threat in his tone and she knew that he hadn't forgotten that day when he had seen Chris hug her. "Leave Chris alone!" she flared. "He's a good friend."

"I can imagine. He went with you to Washington, didn't he?" Rhy gritted savagely, abruptly catching her wrist and pulling her against him. "And he's the one you went to the airport to see off, isn't he?"

"Yes, he is," she admitted, surprised that he should remember that. She tried to release her wrist, and he anchored her to him with his other arm, sliding it about her waist.

"Here's another warning for you," he ground out. "You're still my wife and I won't tolerate another man in your bed. I don't care how long we've been separated. If I catch him with you I'm going to push his teeth through the back of his head and then I'm going to take it up with you. Is that what you want? Are you trying to push me into proving how much I want you?" Without waiting for an answer he bent his head and ground his mouth against hers, forcing a response from her and parting her lips to allow his deeper kiss.

The familiar taste of his mouth tore away the years that had separated them, and she gasped at the lash of desire that sent her hands up to cling to his heavy shoulders as she pressed herself to him. It was their first kiss all over again. She melted, and her awareness of the world around her faded. Even as she responded to him she writhed inside with shame that she didn't have more self-respect than to be so vulnerable to him. He'd never really cared about her, he'd admitted it, but he liked going to bed with her, and she was too weak to resist him. It was odd that no other man had ever tempted her as Rhy did, but then, she'd never known another man like him. He was hard and brutal, but he was strong, and the force of his personality swept lesser people to the side.

But their attraction wasn't all one-sided, she realized dazedly a moment later when his hard hands slid down to her waist and clenched almost painfully on her soft flesh as he pulled her even closer to his taut frame. He groaned against her lips and a tremor rocked through him. "Sallie," he muttered, lifting his mouth a scant inch from hers. "Let's go to my apartment. We can't make love here, there are too many interruptions." His voice was a low growl, rough with his passion, and she shivered in sensual reaction.

"Let me go," she protested, her hands suddenly finding the strength to push against him as panic flared with the realization that it might be impossible to control him now. Their brief marriage had given her an intimate knowledge of his nature and now she admitted to herself that she'd forgotten none of it. She knew by the dark flush on his cheekbones, the timbre of his voice, the dilated glitter of his eyes, that he was half-wild with desire, near the point where he would take her regardless of where they were.

"No," he denied, his mouth twisting savagely. "I told you I'll never let you go."

She fought her way out of his embrace, but she had the uneasy feeling that he'd allowed her to gain her freedom, and spots of color also stained her face as she stared at him. "You'll have to," she told him fiercely. "I don't want you anymore!"

"I just proved you wrong in that!" he said on a short bark of laughter.

"I'm not talking about sex! I don't want to live with you. I don't want to be your wife. I can't stop you from traveling with me, you're the boss, but I won't sleep with you."

"Won't you?" he murmured. "You're my wife, and I want you back. Legally you can't refuse me my marital rights."

His determination, the steel in his gray eyes, alarmed her and she stepped back from him. Desperately she seized on Chris, throwing his name up like a shield to hide behind. "Look, Rhy, you're an adult, surely you can understand that my affections are elsewhere. Chris is special to me—"

A little muscle in his jaw began to twitch and she stared at it in fascination, forgetting what she'd been about to say. Rhy's hands closed painfully on her waist again and he ground out, "I told you what I'd do if I caught him with you and I meant it."

"Be reasonable," she implored, pulling vainly at his hands in an effort to ease the painful pressure. "For heaven's sake, I'm not demanding that you terminate your relationship with Coral!"

An odd expression crossed his face. "No, you're not, are you?" he said slowly.

He looked down at her with growing menace and to escape the impression she had of a time bomb ticking its way to the moment of explosion she managed a casual laugh. "I never thought that you'd live the life of a monk all these years." She tried to soothe the temper in him. "I've no right to object in any event."

Instead of soothing him her words seemed to inflame him more, and the tension in his arms lifted her on her toes. "I'm not that modern and open-minded," he said almost soundlessly, his taut lips barely moving. "I don't want another man touching you!"

"Isn't that a dog-in-the-manger attitude?" she hurled at him and winced in pain as his fingers clenched. "Rhy, please! You're hurting me!"

He cursed vividly, then moved his hands from her waist in the manner of one freeing a bird and she swiftly moved a couple of steps from him, her hands automatically massaging her aching flesh. As he merely stood there watching her and made no move to break the silence that fell between them she decided that the best thing she could do was to get out of there. She couldn't handle Rhy when he was angry, he could reduce her to putty if he really lost his temper and she knew him well enough to know that he was on the verge of violence.

She edged toward the door and he moved suddenly, placing himself between her and her escape. "Don't fight me," he warned, still in that soft, nearly soundless voice. "You can't win and I don't want to hurt you. You're mine, Sallie."

Fear edged along her nerves. She'd seen Rhy in a lot of moods, in a lot of tempers, but she'd never before seen him with this wild savagery in his eyes. "I need to go to work," she muttered warily, watching him for any movement.

"You work for me. You go when I say you can go." He bit out the words, his eyes locked on hers, and she was helpless to look away. Was this how a snake paralyzed a bird?

Desperately she searched her mind for something to say that would break his concentration on her, but nothing surfaced and she squared her shoulders, ready to make a flight of it if necessary. She wouldn't be molested, not even by her own husband! All of the pride and dignity that she'd so painstakingly amassed for herself was in the tilt of her chin as she raised it at him. "Don't push me," she warned him evenly. "If you're even half the man you used to be you know that I'm not willing."

"You would be, after a minute," he retorted with brutal truth, but not by a flicker of her lashes did she betray the jolt he gave her with that statement.

"Don't confuse the past with the future. The days are long gone when I thought the sun rose and set on you."

"Good," he said, his mouth twisting. "I never wanted to be an idol. But don't make me out to be a villain, either."

With inner relief Sallie sensed that the danger was past, at least for the moment. She was tempted to try arguing with him about the trip to Sakarya, but she knew better than to provoke his temper again. "I really do need to get to work," she insisted.

After a moment he stepped to one side. "All right," he permitted, his tone at once tender and warning. "But we're not finished, baby, and when you go to Sakarya I'll be with you every inch of the way."

With that warning ringing in her head Sallie slipped past him and returned to her desk. She began trembling with delayed reaction and with difficulty she tried to concentrate on her writing. But she'd reached a slow spot. She couldn't decide just how the action should go and eventually her thoughts wandered back to Rhy.

Once she would have been delirious with joy if he'd announced that he wanted her with him, wanted her to have his children, but that was a long time ago, and she'd been a different person then. Why couldn't he accept that? Why was he so insistent on resuming their marriage?

She couldn't believe that he was motivated by jealousy. It had to be that possessiveness of his, because jealousy indicated caring, and she knew that Rhy had never loved her, not even in the early days. Their only bond had been a sexual one and he wanted to renew that bond now, but she was determined to break the weakness that made her respond to him.

Then the thought occurred to her that it was one thing to be an ordinary, quiet, stay-at-home little housewife and quite another for her to be a globetrotting, successful reporter. She was more of a feather in his cap now, wasn't she? She hadn't been glamorous enough for him before! Was that why he was suddenly so interested after years of neglect? Rage burned in her for a moment; then she had the disquieting thought that if that was the case he wouldn't have grounded her, he'd have kept her in the limelight.

She didn't understand him; she'd never understand him. Why didn't he leave her alone?

It had to be the tension caused by her scene with Rhy that produced the pounding headache she had that afternoon when she went home. She wanted nothing more than peace and quiet, so she indulged herself with a hot bath and, rather than get dressed afterward, she merely pulled on her comfortable pink robe which zipped up to her throat and sat down at her typewriter to work her way out of the doldrums.

It was still early, not yet seven, when her doorbell rang and she frowned irritably as she switched the typewriter off. Just as she reached the door she thought better of opening it in case Rhy had decided to press his attentions. "Who is it?" she asked warily.

"Coral Williams" was the cool reply and Sallie's eyebrows rose in silent astonishment as she unlocked the door and opened it.

"Come in," she invited the striking blonde, then indicated her robe with a movement of her hand. "I'm sorry about the way I'm dressed, but I wasn't expecting visitors."

"No, that's true enough," Coral admitted, walking into the apartment with the prowling slink of a model. She was both cool and dramatic, dressed in a lemon yellow evening gown that should have made her hair look brassy but didn't. "Rhy is taking me to a Broadway opening, so I knew he wouldn't be here tonight."

Aha! Sallie thought to herself. It looked as if Coral was checking out the competition, but who had told her? "He isn't likely to be here any other night either," she denied, and the amusement in her eyes and voice must have gotten through to Coral because the woman bit her lip and flushed.

"Don't try to hide it from me," she said huskily, her voice growing thick as if she was near tears. "Rhy told me himself."

"What?" Sallie's voice rose in astonishment. Was Rhy going to start advertising their marriage? Did he think that public knowledge might weaken her stand?

"I know how hard it is to resist Rhy when he decides that he wants a woman," Coral was saying. "Believe me, I know! But you're not in his league and he'll only hurt you. He's had other women, but he's always come back to me and this time won't be any different. I just thought I'd let you know before you get in too deeply with him."

"Thanks for the warning," Sallie said, her inner amusement breaking out in a smile that made Coral look at her in disbelief. She couldn't help it; she thought it was funny that her husband's mistress should warn her about becoming too serious about him! "But I don't think you have anything to worry about. I'm not interested in having an affair with anyone, and you'll be doing me a favor if you can keep Rhy's attention away from me."

"How I'd like to!" Coral admitted wryly, glancing at Sallie with disturbing honesty. "But I knew when I first saw you that Rhy was interested, and he won't give up easily. Why do you think he's going on this Sakarya trip with you? If I were you, and if you're on the level about not wanting an affair with him, I'd check into the hotel bookings, because if I know Rhy there'll only be one room available!"

"I know that," Sallie chuckled, "and I'm ahead of him. I've already thought of another place to stay. With a friend." She didn't add that the friend was Marina Delchamp and that she hoped to stay in the palace. She was fairly certain that Marina would offer her sanctuary and would, in fact, greatly enjoy helping her to thwart Rhy.

Suddenly Coral laughed. "Maybe I was worried about nothing. You seem more than capable of looking after yourself. It must be that braid that makes you look so young."

"Probably," Sallie agreed blandly, thinking that in all probability she was Coral's age.

"You've set my mind at ease, so I'll leave now. Rhy is supposed to meet me in half an hour and I'll probably be late." Coral glided to the door and Sallie opened it for her, feeling rather like a servant opening a door for a queen, but laughter still lurked in her eyes as she returned to her writing. Coral acting concerned for another woman was a performance worth watching! Not for a second did she believe that the beautiful model cared a snap of her fingers about another woman's feelings. What Coral so carefully guarded was Rhy's attention, his time, and with a shake of her head Sallie wondered what made Rhy so sinfully attractive.

Perhaps if she knew what made her so vulnerable to Rhy she'd be able to fight him, but she could pinpoint no concrete reason. It was everything about him, even the qualities that made her so angry. He was all man, the only man she'd ever wanted.

Realization struck and the force of it made her break out in a cold sweat, but she forced herself to admit the truth. She still loved him; she always had. She had tried to push her love away in self-defense against the crippling pain she'd felt when Rhy had left her, but she hadn't been able to kill it. It had flourished in the darkness of her subconscious and now she could no longer deny that it existed. She sat at the typewriter, staring blankly at the keys, and let the knowledge creep into her consciousness. She couldn't stop the tears that welled in her eyes, though she stubbornly refused to let them fall. Love was one thing, but compatibility was quite another, and she was no longer a starry-eyed young girl who believed that love could conquer all. She and Rhy were the mismatch of the century, even more so now than in the beginning.

At least then she'd thought him the center of the universe and would gladly have followed him into the jaws of death if he'd only asked her.

But he hadn't asked her; he'd gone alone, disregarding her fears and clinging timidity. When had he ever cared how she felt? He was too forceful, too self-confident, to put her opinion, her feelings, above his own. It had been that way then and it was still the same. Wasn't that how he was acting now? What she wanted just didn't count! Look at the high-handed manner in which he'd stopped her career in its tracks and demanded that she resume their married life. What about her plans, what she wanted out of life?

Drawing several deep breaths, Sallie tried to force her thoughts into order. If she went back to Rhy what would she have? The answer was simple, she would have Rhy—for as long as he remained interested. Or perhaps she wouldn't even have his undivided attention at all. She couldn't discount Coral Williams, and Rhy had never promised fidelity. He'd made no promises at all, other than ones of physical pleasure. So, if she went back to him, she'd have sensual satisfaction and what joy she could find in his company.

On the other side of the coin, what would he gain from a reconciliation? Once again, the first thing that came to mind was sex. That fierce attraction was mutual, unfortunately, for it made him unreasonable. If Coral was pushing him for a commitment Sallie's return would put a stop to that particular demand, and from what Coral had just told her Rhy wouldn't have any worries that Coral might leave him. No, Coral would stay for as long as Rhy wanted her, and if he could have both women at once he probably would.

Sallie winced from that thought. No, Rhy wasn't like that. She didn't think him capable of fidelity to any one woman, but he didn't play games. A woman had to accept him as he was. That had been their trouble. She'd wanted him to be something he wasn't: an ordinary husband. Rhy had refused to change, or even compromise.

So she'd changed, slipped out from under his thumb, and he resented that even while she challenged him. She'd belonged to him once and he couldn't tolerate the idea that she no longer wanted to. That possessive streak of his had to be a mile wide. She'd been his once, and he wanted her back, and he'd move heaven and earth to get her, even if he had to destroy her career to do so.

She *couldn't* go back to him, though deep down she craved to do just that. Her own identity was at stake. Rhy would swamp her, smother her. Then, when he was no longer interested, he'd walk out, and she didn't think she could survive that again.

No, she had to follow her own path, and if it led her away from Rhy she had to accept that. Odd how she could love him and yet be willing to spend her life separated from him, yet that was the way of it. She knew instinctively that Rhy would destroy her sense of self, her confidence, if she allowed him control over her emotions again.

There was no hesitation; she had to choose the path that was right for her, and that path didn't include Rhy. Perhaps no other man would ever make her heart pound madly as the lightest touch from Rhy could do, but if that was the price, she'd pay it. She had to.

When this trip to Sakarya was over she would turn in her notice and leave town. She couldn't wait any longer. Rhy was closing in, and she'd have to keep her guard up every minute.

Chapter Six

The night before they were due to leave for Sakarya Sallie went to bed early, hoping that she'd be able to get to sleep since the flight would be long and she'd never been able to rest on a trip. She was always too keyed up, too restless, and to her dismay she felt the same way now. The thought of traveling with Rhy, when every self-preserving instinct in her screamed to keep as far away from him as she could, had all her nerves tingling in mingled fear and expectation. It was rather like petting a beautiful tiger, wanting so desperately to touch something so lovely but knowing at the same time that the tiger could kill you.

She turned restlessly in the bed, tangling the sheets, and when the doorbell rang she jumped out of bed with a sense of relief and grabbed her robe, shrugging into it as she ran to the door. Just as she reached it she skidded to a stop and called, "Who is it?"

"Chris," came a muffled voice and Sallie's brow knit in puzzlement. What was he doing here? He'd been on the road a lot lately, due to Rhy's influence, no doubt, but he'd arrived back in town the day before, and he'd been fine earlier when she'd seen him long enough to say a quick hello. Now he sounded as if he was sick, or in pain.

Quickly she unlocked the various locks on the door and opened it. Chris had been slumped against the doorframe, and he straightened, giving her a glimpse of his drawn face. "What's wrong?" she asked swiftly, catching his sleeve and pulling him in so she could close the door. She fumbled with the locks again, then turned to him. He'd jammed his hands deep into his pockets and stood regarding her with deep, silent misery evident in his brown eyes.

Sallie caught her breath. Had someone been killed? That was always her first thought, her deepest fear. She held out her hand to him and he took it, squeezing her slender fingers in a painful grip. "What is it?" she asked softly. "Chris?"

"I didn't know it would hurt so bad," he groaned, his voice so low that she could barely hear him. "Oh, God, Sallie, I didn't know."

"Who is it?" she demanded, grasping his arm urgently with her free hand. "Chris Meaker, if you don't tell me—"

He shook his head as if to clear it, as if he'd abruptly realized what she thought. "No," he said thinly. "No one's dead, unless you want to count me. She's left me, Sallie."

Sallie gaped at him, remembering that he was in love with a woman who wanted the same things she'd once wanted, a nice, normal husband who came home every night, who fathered children and loved them and was around to see them grow up. Evidently the woman had decided that she couldn't live with Chris's job, with knowing that every trip could be his last one. Granted, some of the assignments weren't that dangerous, but it was a high-risk job at best. She hadn't been able to take it, either, the constant worry about someone she loved desperately. Only by cutting Rhy out of her life had she been able to function again.

"What can I do?" she asked in quiet sympathy. "Tell me how to help."

"Tell me it'll get better," he begged, and his voice cracked. "Sallie, hold me. Please, hold me!" To her horror his face twisted and he began to sob, jerking her to him with desperate arms and holding her so tightly that she couldn't breathe. His entire body was shaking and he buried his face in her neck, wetting her skin and hair and collar with his salty tears. Great tearing sobs tore from him and she put her arms around him, giving him what he'd asked for, someone to hold him. She knew what he was feeling; dear God, she knew exactly what he was going through.

She'd cried that way for Rhy, feeling as if he'd torn her insides out and she'd die from the pain of it.

"It'll get better," she promised thickly, tears blurring her own voice. "I know, Chris. I've been there."

He didn't answer, but his arms lifted her, taking her from the floor. He drew a deep, shuddering breath and swallowed, trying to control himself. "God knows it can't get any worse," he whispered, and lifted his head. For a moment his brown eyes, wet and miserable, stared into her wet blue ones, and then he dipped his head and fastened his mouth to hers, kissing her with silent desperation. Sallie understood and she kissed him back. He wasn't kissing her for any sexual reason; it was merely a reaching out for human contact, a plea for comforting. She'd always liked Chris; at that moment she came to love him. Not the deep, ravenous love she had for Rhy, not even a man-woman type of love. She simply loved him as a human being, a fellow creature who was vulnerable and who needed her. She'd never been needed in her life before; she'd been dependent on her parents, then dependent on Rhy. Certainly Rhy had never needed her!

Chris pulled his head back and sighed; then he rested his forehead against hers. "What can I do?" he asked, but she knew that he didn't expect an answer. "How long does it take?"

Now that she *could* answer. "It took me a couple of months before I could even begin to function again," she told him truthfully, and he winced. "But I worked at getting over it harder than I've ever worked at anything in my life, either before or since."

"I can't believe she did it," he groaned.

"Did you have a fight?" Sallie asked, leading him to the sofa and pushing until he sat down heavily.

His head moved wearily back and forth. "No fight. Not even an ultimatum. My God, you'd think she'd at least give me a warning! If she wanted to tear my guts out she bull's-eyed first shot!"

Sitting down beside him, Sallie took his hand and held it. With the insight of someone who had been there, she felt that she understood very well the motives of Chris's unnamed lady. He thought it was perfectly all right for him to risk life and limb while she waited patiently at home for him—how much warning did he think she'd have of his death? Did he think the pain would be any less for her if she was suddenly told that he hadn't made it back? Men were so arrogant and selfish, even Chris, and he was one of the most likeable people she'd ever met. Aloud she said, "Don't expect someone to give in just because you can't. You'd have made each other miserable. Face it, you're better off apart."

"I've never loved anyone before," he protested hopelessly. "It's not so easy to give up someone you really love!"

"I did, and I didn't have a choice either. He left me flat on my face."

Chris sighed and stared at the pattern of the carpet, and Sallie could read his anguish in the lines of his face. Chris had always seemed younger than his years, as if life had passed within touching distance of him but had never actually touched him, glancing off his inner calm like light off of a mirror. Now he'd aged and the boyishness was gone from his face.

"Her name is Amy," he said abruptly. "She's quiet, a little shy. I guess it took me a year of chance meetings in the hallways before she'd do more than smile at me when I spoke. Then it took me another year to get her into bed—" He stopped and glanced at her, his mouth going grim. "Forget I said that. I don't usually kiss and tell."

"It's forgotten," Sallie assured him. "Did you ask her to marry you?"

"Not at first. I've never wanted to be married, Sal, I'm a lone wolf, like you." He shook his head as if he didn't understand himself. "It kind of sneaked up on me, the idea of getting married. So finally I asked her and she cried. She said she loved me but that she couldn't take my job, and she'd marry me if I changed jobs. Hell, I love my job! Mexican standoff."

"And she cut her losses," Sallie murmured.

"She also hedged her bets." He gave her a wry, self-mocking smile. "She had another game going with a nine-to-five guy. She told me tonight that they're getting married later this year."

"Is she bluffing?"

Chris shook his head. "I don't think so. She's wearing a diamond."

After sitting quietly for a moment Sallie said frankly, "You've got a choice, you know. You can have Amy or you can have your job, but you can't have both. Decide which one's the most important to you and forget about the other."

"Did you forget about your guy when you chose your job over him?" challenged Chris.

"You've got it wrong. I was in Amy's shoes, not yours. He chose *his* job over *me*," said Sallie. "I've never forgotten him, but I've done very well without him, thank you."

It wasn't until Chris spoke that she realized how much information she'd given him with her stray comments; or perhaps it was just that Chris was intuitive, sensing her moods and thoughts without any concrete evidence. After looking at her thoughtfully for a moment he murmured, "It's Baines, isn't it? He's the one who walked out on you."

Her stunned expression had to tell him the answer, but after a minute she gathered herself enough to admit, "He's the one. And let me tell you, when Rhy Baines walks, he walks *hard!*"

"He's a fool," Chris said mildly. "But he wants you back, doesn't he?"

"Not permanently," Sallie replied with a touch of bitterness. "He just wants to play for a while."

Chris looked at her for a long time, his brown eyes moving over her small face, shuttered now to keep from revealing any more of her inner pain. When it became evident that she had nothing more to say he leaned forward and gently kissed her, but this time he was offering comfort instead of taking it. Sallie closed her eyes and let the kiss linger, neither responding nor rejecting but letting time expand as his mouth moved lightly over hers. She'd never been kissed like that before, without passion, as a friend.

The strident demand of the telephone caused Chris to remove his mouth and with a murmured "Excuse me" Sallie stretched to reach the yellow receiver. When she answered she felt a tingle of alarm when a husky voice demanded, "Have you finished packing?"

"Of course," she said crisply, feeling insulted that he felt he had to check up on her. What did he think she'd do, wait until the last minute to throw everything together? Because of that, and also because of a certain streak of feminine perversity, she added, "I was just talking to Chris."

She could feel the thickness of the silence on the line; then the growing crackle of Rhy's anger leapt out at her. "Is he there?" he finally bit out, the words almost exploding from his lips. Sallie had a mental picture of him, his teeth bared in a snarl, his cheekbones taut and savage with his rage. The gray eyes would be flinty, with red sparks snapping in them. The tingle of alarm inside her changed to one almost of pleasure.

"Of course he's here," she responded, knowing that she was flirting with danger. What would she do if Rhy's temper roared out of control? The last thing she wanted to do was cause any trouble for Chris, but somehow Rhy goaded her past responsible actions. "I don't give up my friends just because you snap your fingers,'' she heard herself adding.

His voice was a low growl, almost too low to hear. "When I snap my something it won't be my fingers. Get rid of him, Sallie, and do it now."

Immediately she bristled. "I will not—"

"Now," he whispered. "Or I'm coming over. I'm not playing, baby. Get rid of him. Then come back and tell me you've done it."

Furiously she tossed the receiver onto the table and got to her feet. Without a word, not wanting Rhy to hear anything she said to Chris, she held out her hand to him, and with a puzzled look he took it, rising lightly to his feet. Sallie led him to the door, then stretched on tiptoe and kissed him gently. "I'm sorry," she murmured. "He's ordered me to get rid of you or he's going to come over here and get violent."

For a moment Chris looked like his old self, one eyebrow rising in mild mockery. "This sounds serious. Sallie, old girl, I think you've left a lot out of your story."

"I have, but there's no use in raking over old ashes. Will you be all right?" she asked, concern evident in her voice and eyes, and he quickly hugged her.

"Of course I will. Just telling you helped. Kissing you helped even more." He gave a crooked grin. "She knocked me for a loop, but I'm not giving up. She cried when she told me she's marrying this other guy, so it's not hopeless, is it?''

Sallie grinned back. "Doesn't sound hopeless to me."

He flicked her cheek with one finger. "Have a good time in Sakarya," he teased, and she stuck her tongue out at him. After he'd gone she carefully locked the door and returned to glare balefully at the telephone receiver lying there waiting for her. She was tempted to let him wait a few more minutes, but it was like a dose of bitter medicine: soonest done, soonest over with.

With that thought she snatched it up and nearly snarled, "Well, he's gone!"

"What took you so long?" he barked in demand.

"I was kissing him goodbye!" she retorted furiously. "And now I'm *telling you* goodbye!"

"Don't hang up," came the soft warning. "I'm going to give Meaker just enough time to get home, then I'm going to call and make sure he's there. For your sake, you'd better pray that he goes straight home."

"Your bully act is getting boring," she snapped, and slammed the phone down, then unplugged it. Marching into her bedroom she unplugged that phone too, but not before it began ringing. Muttering furiously to herself about what she'd like to do to Rhy Baines, she stomped around the apartment turning off lights, then flung herself on the bed and once again tried to go to sleep. If it had been difficult before it was impossible now. She was burning with righteous indignation, and she wondered how anyone could be such a hypocrite. It was perfectly all right for him to blatantly carry on his affair with Coral right in front of her, but he had no intention of allowing her the same freedom. Not that she wanted to have an affair with Chris any more than he wanted one with her, but that was beside the point.

Then her thoughts turned to the trip to Sakarya. After tonight Rhy would be his most demanding, his most seductive, and to her dismay she recalled that in the past he'd had no difficulty at all in getting her to bed. She'd been lucky that, since he'd discovered her identity, the only times he'd kissed her they had been in his office where there had been scant opportunity for a seduction scene; she had her doubts that she'd have been so successful in stopping him otherwise. She was too honest to delude herself even when the truth was painful. She loved Rhy, but even if she didn't she'd still want him physically. Only her pride and her deep-rooted fear of being hurt again kept her from giving in to him.

It was after midnight before she finally drifted into sleep and the flight to Paris, the first leg of the trip to Sakarya, was an early one. She was pale with weariness before she even left her apartment to meet Rhy at the air terminal. She was determined to be as businesslike as possible, both to keep him at a distance and to show him that he hadn't upset her with his jealous rage of the night before, but right from the start her attitude was difficult to maintain. When he saw her walking toward him Rhy got to his feet and came to meet her, taking her larger tote bag from her arm and bending down to press a brief warm kiss on her lips. "Good morning," he murmured, letting his dark gray eyes drift down over her body. "I like you in a dress. You should wear one more often."

So he was going to ignore last night, was he? Though she'd intended to do the same thing she felt a flare of irritation that he'd beaten her to the punch. Then she shrugged mentally and gave him a cool glance. "I thought the Sakaryans would prefer dresses over pants." She usually wore pants while traveling both for comfort and convenience, but considering the nature of the assignment she'd packed only dresses. For the flight she'd chosen a lightweight beige dress, sleeveless, with a low-scooped neckline, but the dress also had a matching long-sleeved jacket, and she was wearing it now, for despite the heat of summer in New York City she often felt cool in the early mornings, and she'd learned from experience that the temperature-controlled jetliners were too cool for her. She had also changed her hair from the informal braid to a neat coil on the back of her head. There wasn't a lot she could do with her hair, because of its length, but for more formal gatherings she always put it up.

"I also prefer dresses," he commented, taking her arm. "You have great legs, and I like to see them. You used to wear dresses a lot, as I remember."

That's right, remind me, she thought savagely, but she managed to give him an impersonal answer. "When I started working I found that pants are more suitable for the type of work I do." To change the subject she questioned, "Do you have the tickets?"

"Everything's taken care of," he assured her. "Do you want a cup of coffee before the flight's called?"

"No, thanks. I don't drink coffee while I'm traveling," she felt compelled to explain, and took a seat in an armchair. The glint in his gray eyes as he seated himself opposite her told her that Rhy was well aware why she hadn't chosen the sofa, but she ignored him and amused herself by watching the parade of early-morning travelers.

Their flight was five minutes late, and Rhy was already restless when the loudspeaker called their flight number. He got to his feet and took her arm, and suddenly he gave her a whimsical smile. "Those are some spikes you're wearing," he commented. "You come up to my chin... almost."

"They're also dangerous weapons," she said, her mouth curving.

"Are they? Are you planning to use them on me?" he asked, and before she could turn her mouth away he swooped his head down and captured her lips in a hard, hungry kiss that took her breath away.

"Rhy, please!" she protested, determined to hide the curling response she felt whenever he touched her. "We're in public!"

"I get more chances to touch you in public than I do in private, so I'm going to take advantage of them," he muttered in warning.

"This is business!" she hissed. "Try to remember that. It won't do the magazine any good if a reporter acts badly in public."

"No one here knows you're a reporter," he retorted with a grin. "Besides, I'm your boss and I say it's okay."

"I have standards, even if you don't, and I don't like being pawed! Are you going to catch this flight or not?"

"I wouldn't miss it for the world," he drawled, and she caught his hidden meaning and flushed. Beyond any doubt Rhy was planning on a reconciliation during this trip, and she was equally determined to prevent such a thing from happening. Marina would never turn her away, she was certain, and she relished the thought of Rhy's fury when he found she'd evaded him.

But for now she faced a long flight in his company and she didn't relish *that*. Not only did his presence make her nervous, she was a restless traveler under the best of circumstances. Before they'd been in the air an hour she'd flipped through several magazines and made a stab at reading a paperback she'd brought with her, then abandoned that for a book of crossword puzzles. When she discarded that and tried reading her book again Rhy reached out and took her hand.

"Relax," he advised, rubbing his thumb across the back of her hand, a gesture guaranteed to keep her from relaxing. "It's a long flight, and you're as jumpy as a flea. You'll be worn-out before we get to Paris, let alone Sakarya."

"I'm not a good traveler," she admitted. "I'm not good at sitting still with nothing to do." Already she was bored, and she yearned for her manuscript, but she'd been afraid to risk losing it, so she had left it behind.

"Try to take a nap," he advised. "You'll need it."

"I can't do that, either," she said with a rueful grin. "I'm just nervous enough of heights that I don't trust the pilot enough to go to sleep and let him handle it all."

"I didn't know you were afraid of heights," he said, and she bristled.

"I'm not afraid, I'm nervous. There's a difference. I fly all the time—or *used* to—and I've been in plenty of tight spots without going to pieces. I've even enjoyed some of them. In fact, I once took a few flying lessons, but that's another thing I didn't have the time to keep up."

"You've been busy," he said on an odd note. "What other accomplishments have you added since we parted company?"

He seemed to resent that and she suddenly felt proud that she had accomplished so much. At least he'd know that she hadn't been pining for him. "I speak six foreign languages, three fluently," she enumerated coolly. "I'm a fair shot, and I've learned how to stay on a horse. I've had to give up a lot of things I've tried—and that includes cooking and sewing, because I realized how boring they were. Anything else?"

"I hope not," he retorted, his mouth quivering with amusement. "No wonder Downey sent you into so many hot spots, you probably bullied him into it!"

"Greg can't be bullied, he's tough as nails," Sallie defended her editor. "And he'd be in the field himself if he could."

"Why can't he? I remember him as one of the best, but he suddenly grounded himself, and I've never heard why."

"He was shot up pretty badly in Vietnam," Sallie explained. "And while he was recovering his wife died of a stroke. It was quite a shock, there'd been no warning at all, but all of a sudden she was dead. They had two children, a boy and a girl, and the little girl had a hard time adjusting to her mother's death, so Greg decided to stay home with the kids."

"That's rough," Rhy commented.

"He doesn't talk about it much."

"But he told you?" he asked sharply.

"In bits and pieces. Like I said, he doesn't talk about it much."

"A field reporter doesn't need a family. The old Pony Express advertised for riders who were orphans and had no family ties, and I sometimes think that should hold true for reporters, too."

"I agree," she said sharply, not looking at him. "That's why I don't want any ties."

HARLEQUIN®

AN IMPORTANT MESSAGE
FROM
THE EDITORS

Dear Reader,

Because you've chosen to read one of
"The Best of the Best", we'd like to say
"thank you"! And, as a **special** way to
thank you, we've selected <u>three more</u> of the
<u>books</u> you love so well, **and** a Victorian
Picture Frame to send you absolutely *FREE!*

Please enjoy them with our compliments...

Editor,
The Best of the Best

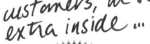

*P.S. And because we value our
customers, we've attached something
extra inside ...*

EDITOR'S
**FREE
GIFT
SEAL**
THANK YOU

PEEL OFF SEAL AND
PLACE INSIDE

HOW TO VALIDATE
YOUR
EDITOR'S FREE GIFT
"THANK YOU"

1. Peel off gift seal from front cover. Place it in space provided at right. This automatically entitles you to receive three free books and a lovely pewter-finish Victorian Picture Frame.

2. Send back this card and you'll get 3 of "The Best of the Best™" novels. These books have a cover price of $4.50 each, but they are yours to keep absolutely free.

3. There's no catch. You're under no obligation to buy anything. We charge nothing—ZERO—for your first shipment. And you don't have to make any minimum number of purchases—not even one!

4. We call this line "The Best of the Best" because each month you'll receive the best books by the world's hottest romance authors. These are authors whose names show up time and again on all the major bestseller lists and whose books sell out as soon as they hit the stores. You'll love getting them conveniently delivered to your home...and you'll love our discount prices.

5. We hope that after receiving your free books you'll want to remain a subscriber. But the choice is yours—to continue or cancel, anytime at all! So why not take us up on our invitation, with no risk of any kind. You'll be glad you did!

6. Don't forget to detach your FREE BOOKMARK. And remember...just for validating your Editor's Free Gift Offer, we'll send you FOUR MORE gifts, *ABSOLUTELY FREE!*

YOURS FREE!
*This lovely Victorian pewter-finish miniature is perfect for displaying a treasured photograph—and it's yours **absolutely free**—when you accept our no-risk offer!*

PLACE
FREE GIFT
SEAL
HERE

YES!

I have placed my Editor's "thank you" seal in the space provided above. Please send me 3 free books and a Victorian picture frame. I understand I am under no obligation to purchase any books, as explained on the back and on the opposite page.

183 CIH ANCV (U-BB-01/94)

_____

NAME

_____

ADDRESS   APT.

_____

CITY   STATE   ZIP

Thank you!

THE BEST OF THE BEST™: HERE'S HOW IT WORKS

Accepting free books puts you under no obligation to buy anything. You may keep the books and gift and return the shipping statement marked "cancel." If you do not cancel, about a month later we will send you 3 additional novels, and bill you just $3.74 each plus 25¢ delivery and applicable sales tax, if any.* That's the complete price, and—compared to cover prices of $4.50 each—quite a bargain! You may cancel at any time, but if you choose to continue,every month we'll send you 3 more books, which you may either purchase at the discount price...or return at our expense and cancel your subscription.

*Terms and prices subject to change without notice. Sales tax applicable in N.Y.

"But you're not a reporter any longer," he murmured, his long fingers tightening around her hand. "Consider this your swan song, because after this your position will be that of Mrs. Rhydon Baines."

Swiftly Sallie jerked her hand away from him and stared out at the cloud cover below them. "Are you firing me?" she bit out angrily.

"I will if you force me to. I don't mind if you work so long as you're home every night with me. Of course, when we have children I'll want you to be home with them while they're small."

She turned furious blue eyes on him. "I won't live with you," she said bitterly. "I *can't* live with you and be more than half-alive myself. The thought of being a housewife again is nauseating."

His mouth turned grim. "You're lying to yourself if you believe that. You've changed a lot of things, but you can't change the way you feel about children. I remember how you were when you were pregnant with our son—"

"Shut up!" she flared, her fingers curving into her palms as she strove to control her pain at the memory of her dead child. "Don't talk about my baby." Even after seven years the pain of losing him was raw and unhealed, and for the rest of her life she would mourn that small, lost life.

"My son, too," Rhy said tightly.

"Really?" she challenged, lowering her voice to keep others from hearing her. "You weren't there when I gave birth, and you were seldom home during my pregnancy. The only role you played was to physically father the baby. After that, I was on my own.'' She turned away, swallowing in an effort to control the tears that threatened as she remembered her son. She'd never heard him cry, never watched him look about at the strange new world he'd entered, but for several magic months she'd felt his movements as he kicked and turned inside her and he'd been real to her, a person, and he'd had a name. She had somehow known she would have a boy, and he had been David Rhydon Baines, her son.

Rhy's fingers closed over her wrist so tightly that the fragile bones ground together and she winced with pain. "I wanted him, too," Rhy ground out, then almost flung her wrist aside. The next several hours passed in silence.

There was no layover in Paris and Sallie guessed that Greg had made the arrangements, because he always arranged things as tightly as he could, sometimes resulting in a missed flight when the first flight was only a little late. She and Rhy had barely checked through customs when their connecting flight was called, and they had to run to make the plane. From Paris it was another seven hours before they landed at the new, ultramodern jetport in Khalidia, the capital of Sakarya, and because of the time change, instead of the night their bodies were ready for, they were thrown into the middle of the Sakaryan day.

Their weariness and the long hours had largely erased the constraint between them, and Sallie didn't protest when he took her arm as they walked across the tarmac to the low, sprawling air terminal. The heat was incredible, and she was actually grateful for Rhy's support.

"I hope the hotel's decent," Rhy muttered beneath his breath, "but the way I feel right now I don't care what it's like as long as I can catch some sleep."

She knew the feeling. Jet lag was worse than simply missing sleep, it was total drain. She certainly wasn't up to battling with Rhy over where she would sleep!

They couldn't find anyone who spoke English, but several of the Sakaryans spoke French and both she and Rhy knew that language well. The taxi driver who took them to the hotel in a remarkably battered Renault spoke a rough French, and from what he said they gathered that Khalidia was being overrun by Westerners. Many Europeans had already arrived, and many Americans, including a man with a big camera, and it was said that the King would be on American television. He did not have a television himself, but he had seen one, and he thought that the big camera was one used for making the pictures for the television.

He was talkative, as taxi drivers the world over seemed to be, and he pointed with pride to the gleaming new buildings existing alongside ancient structures baked white by the merciless sun. Sakarya had the intriguing blend of old and new that so many developing nations displayed, with gleaming Mercedes limousines purring up and down the same streets used by donkeys. Camels were still used for travel in the

Sakaryan desert, but overhead contrails were left by the sleek, screaming jets of the Sakaryan Royal Air Command.

The King had been educated at Oxford but, despite his absorption of European culture, he was by nature a cautious man, rather resistant to change. The Sakaryan nation was not a new one; it dated back to the day of Muhammad, and the family of Al Mahdi had held the monarchy for over five hundred years. There were deeply ingrained traditions to consider whenever modernization was discussed and for the most part life in Sakarya went on as before. Motorized vehicles were nice, but the Sakaryans had gotten along without them before and would not mind if suddenly there were no more automobiles. The jetport was too noisy and the people who arrived on the big jets had strange customs. However, the big new hospital was a source of pride and the children were eager to attend the new schools.

The man who had accomplished this modernization was the man Marina Delchamp had married, Zain Abdul ibn Rashid, the finance minister of Sakarya and a man of considerable influence with the King. He was a dark, hawklike man with the coal black eyes of his race, and he'd been an international playboy since his college days in Europe. Sallie wondered if he loved Marina or was attracted only to her shining blond beauty. Did Zain Abdul ibn Rashid cherish Marina's gallant spirit, her natural dignity?

She worried over her thoughts like a terrier, for it wasn't easy for East to meet West. The cultural differences were so vast. Despite their spasmodic correspondence and the long intervals between their meetings Sallie considered Marina a true friend and she wanted her to be happy. She became so engrossed with her worries that she forgot to watch the scenery and was startled when the driver said in French, "The Hotel Khalidia. It is new and rich. You like it, yes?"

Peering around Rhy's shoulder Sallie admitted that she liked it, yes. The hotel was shielded on three sides by a row of carefully nurtured trees and beyond the trees was a high rock wall. The architecture wasn't ultramodern; instead, every effort had been made to insure that the hotel blended with its surroundings. The inside might offer every modern convenience, and she sincerely hoped it did, but the outer facade could have been ageless; it was clean and uncluttered in line, built of gleaming white stone, with deeply recessed windows.

Trying to keep up with Rhy, Sallie found that she was ignored when she tried to explain which cases were hers and which belonged to Rhy. A black-eyed young man in Western dress gave his attention solely to Rhy, not even glancing at her, and she received the same treatment from the desk clerk. The young man disappeared with their luggage and Rhy pocketed the room key.

When they were a few steps away from the desk clerk Sallie caught Rhy's arm. "I want a room of my own," she insisted, looking him in the eye.

"Sorry. I've registered us as man and wife and you'll have a hard time persuading an Islamic man to give you another room," he informed her with evident satisfaction. "You knew what to expect when you came on this trip."

"What do I have to say to get it through you head—" she began in frustration, and he cut her short.

"Later. This isn't the place for a public argument. Stop being difficult, all I want is a shower and a few hours' sleep. Believe me, you're perfectly safe right now."

She didn't believe him, but she had to retrieve her luggage, so she followed him into the elevator, and he punched the button for the fourth floor.

Even as tired as she was the charm of the room made her catch her breath and she barely noticed as Rhy tipped the young man who'd brought up their bags. Though actually only one large room, it was separated by intricate wrought-iron screens in two areas, a sitting room to the front and the bedroom to the rear. A balcony ran the length of the room and it was furnished with two white wicker chairs with thickly padded cushions and a wicker lounger. A small tea table stood between the two chairs. Stepping onto the balcony, she could see the huge swimming pool below, set among palm trees, and she wondered if women were allowed to use the pool.

Returning to the room, she inspected the divan-style bed and smiled at the number of vari-colored cushions that adorned it. The parquet floor was covered in this area by a rug that looked Turkish but was probably a mass-produced copy. That made no difference, the effect was still stunning. Of all the hotels she'd stayed in she already liked this one the best. The food might be terrible, the service nonexistent for all she knew, but she adored the room!

Then she looked up and met Rhy's penetrating gaze and she paled. He'd removed his jacket and his shoulders strained at the material of his white shirt, and something in his stance told her that he was alert to her every movement. "Why don't you take a shower?" he suggested. "I'll make some phone calls and make certain everything's set up for the interview, which could take a while."

She wanted more than anything to grab her suitcases and run, but she knew that Rhy was waiting for just such a move. She would have to trick him and she wasn't certain just yet how to manage it. And a bath sounded like heaven....

"All right," she agreed wearily, picking up her suitcase and taking it into the bathroom that opened off to the right of the sleeping area, carefully locking the door behind her.

Despite her weariness, the bathroom delighted her. It could have come straight out of a Turkish harem with the black-tiled sunken bath, the mosaics, the rich jewel-like colors. She flung her dress off and peeled off her damp underclothing, sighing with relief at the sensation of cool air on her sweaty skin. She turned on the crystal taps that let the water pour into the huge tub and slid with a sigh into the cool water, then splashed about with a fantasy of having servants waiting to help her from the bath and prepare her body with perfumed oils for the coming night with the dark, exciting sultan....

Then reality intruded with the thought that she'd go mad under such circumstances, and she had enough to worry about now without bringing a sultan into it. She got out of the bath and toweled herself dry; then she debated what to wear. If she changed into street clothes Rhy would watch her like a hawk, but she had no intentions of parading around before him in a nightgown. She finally settled on a sapphire blue caftan and zipped herself into it, then took down her hair and brushed it vigorously.

She was too tired to braid it so she left it loose. After picking up her scattered clothing and tidying the bath she unlocked the door and carried her suitcase out.

Rhy was on the phone and he barely looked in her direction as she put belongings away, trying to behave as if she meant to stay. She wandered around the room, fighting to hold off the sleepiness that was growing stronger and listened as Rhy talked to several people.

After some time he covered the mouthpiece with his hand and said to her, "Why don't you go ahead and get some sleep? I don't know how long I'll be."

She didn't want to go to sleep, every instinct screamed against it, but she couldn't leave with him watching her. Besides, she was so tired; every bone and muscle in her ached from the long hours sitting in the plane. She could rest for just a few minutes until Rhy got off the telephone. She was a light sleeper; she'd hear him when he went into the bathroom.

She pulled the shades over the doors to the balcony and dimmed the room into semidarkness, then crawled among the pillows on the divan with a sigh of ecstasy. She stretched out her aching legs, turned her face against a pillow and was instantly asleep.

She was aroused some time later when someone muttered, "Move over," and she rolled over to make room for the warm body that slid next to her. Dimly she was aware that she should wake up, but she was so comfortable and the quiet hum of the central air conditioner lulled her back to sleep.

The time difference was confusing; when she woke it was dark, but she'd slept for hours. Still groggy, she peered at the dim figure coming out of the bathroom. "Who is it?" she called thickly, unable to clear the cobwebs from her mind. She wasn't certain just where she was, either.

"Rhy," the rough-velvet voice answered. "I'm sorry I woke you, I was just getting a drink. Would you like a glass of water, too?"

That sounded heavenly and she sighed a yes, then began struggling into a sitting position. In only a moment a cool glass was being put into her hand and she drained it thirstily, then gave it back to him. He returned the glass to the bathroom as she fell back among the pillows and thought drowsily that he must have eyes like a cat because he hadn't turned on any lights.

Just when the bed dipped beneath his weight again she remembered that she'd been planning on slipping out and her heart lurched with fear. "Wait—" she gasped in panic, reaching out to thrust him away, and her hand encountered smooth warm flesh. Shocked, forgetting what she'd been about to say, instead she blurted out, "You don't have anything on!"

In the darkness he gave a rough chuckle and turned on his side to face her, his heavy arm sliding around her waist and overcoming her futile resistance to pull her snugly against him. "I've always slept in the raw...remember?" he teased, his lips brushing her temple.

Her breath halted in her chest, and she began to tremble at the pressure of his strong, warm body against her. His male scent filled her nostrils and made her senses begin to swim. Desperately fighting her growing need to press herself to him and let him do as he wanted, she put her hands against his chest to push him away and instead found her slim fingers twining in the hair that covered his chest.

"Sallie," he muttered hoarsely, searching for and finding her lips in the darkness, and with a moan she lifted her arms to cling around his neck. She knew she should resist him but that had never been possible and even now, when she had such good reasons for fighting him, the temptation of knowing again such wild satisfaction kept her from shoving him away.

Nor was he unaffected; his big body was trembling against her when he lifted his mouth from hers, scattering kisses across her face and eyes. She felt him slide down the zip of the caftan and pull it from her shoulders, bunching it about her waist, then his shaking hands were exploring the delicately swelling breasts he had bared. Helplessly she buried her face in his shoulder, shuddering with the force of the desire he'd awakened, not wanting him to stop, knowing she'd go mad with frustration if he stopped.

Fiercely he stripped the caftan away from her and threw it aside, and she had a brief moment of sanity as he turned back to her. Her hands clutched at his powerful shoulders and she moaned weakly, "Rhy...don't. We shouldn't."

"You're my wife," he muttered in reply, taking her in his arms again and pressing his weight over her. She gasped at the wild, sweet contact of his bare flesh against hers, then the passion-tart possession of his mouth over hers sucked away her protests, and again her arms lifted and clung about him.

It was as if the years of separation had never been; their bodies were as familiar with each other as they

had been long ago. Caught up in the whirlpool of his
passion she could only respond, only return the passion he so freely gave. He wasn't gentle; except for the
first time, Rhy had never been a gentle lover. He was
fierce, tender, erotic, wildly exciting, and she was unable to stem her passionate reception of his lovemaking. It was just as it had been before—no, it was better;
he drove her beyond sanity, beyond caring, beyond
knowledge of anything except him.

Chapter Seven

Sallie came awake slowly, too comfortable and content to easily relinquish her hold on slumber. She felt utterly boneless, weightless, as if she were afloat. Her body was moving up and down in a gentle rhythm and beneath her head a steady, soothing drum kept time with her heart. She felt so marvelous, so safe....

The shrill ringing of the telephone was a rude interruption into her euphoric state and she muttered a protest. Then her bed moved beneath her and she clutched at it, only to find that instead of sheets her fingers were clinging to hard, warm skin. Her eyes popped open and she raised her head as Rhy stretched out a long, muscular arm and lifted the receiver from the bedside extension. "Hello," he muttered sleepily, his voice even huskier than usual as he wasn't completely awake. He listened a moment, said "Thank you" and hung up, then, with a sigh, closed his eyes again.

Hot color ran into Sallie's cheeks and hastily she tried to scramble away from him and pull up the sheet to cover her nude body. She was prevented from moving by his arms, which tightened about her, holding her in place on his chest. His eyelids, with their thick black lashes, lifted and he surveyed her flushed, tousled, early-morning beauty with a satisfied gleam in his gray eyes.

"Stay here," he commanded huskily. His hand quested down her side, smoothing her silky skin, and he murmured against her ear, "I feel as if I have a kitten curled up on my chest. You hardly weigh anything."

Involuntarily she shivered in delight at his warm breath in her ear, but she made an effort to free herself, saying, "Let me up, Rhy, I want to dress—"

"Not yet, baby," he crooned, brushing her long hair back to press his lips into the small hollow below her ear. "It's still early, and we don't have anything more important to do than getting used to each other again. You're my wife and I like the feel of you in my arms."

"*Estranged* wife," she insisted, trying to arch her head away from his insistent lips, but instead she found herself merely tilting her head back to allow him greater access to her throat. Her heart began pounding when he found the pulse beating at the back of her neck and sucked at it hungrily, as if he wanted to draw her life's blood out of her body.

"We weren't estranged last night," he murmured.

"Last night..." Her voice failed her and after a moment she managed to continue. "Last night was the result of memories, an old attraction, nothing more. Let's just mark it down to auld lang syne and forget about it, shall we?"

He relaxed back against the pillows but kept her cuddled close against him. Surprisingly her statement didn't seem to anger him, for he smiled lazily at her. "It's okay to surrender now," he informed her gently. "I won the war last night."

She almost winced with pain at the thought of giving him up again, yet she knew she couldn't be happy with him now. She let her head fall onto his shoulder and for a moment she allowed herself to relish his closeness. He stroked her back and shoulders, playing with her hair, pulling it all to one side to drift over his chest and shoulder. His touch was sapping her strength, as always, and while she still had the presence of mind she raised her head from the haven of his wide shoulder and gazed at him seriously.

"It still won't work," she whispered. "We've both changed, and there are other considerations now. Coral's in love with you, Rhy. You can't just turn your back on her and hurt her like that—or were you planning on keeping her on the side?"

"You're a little cat," he observed lazily as his hand began questing more intimately, "always scratching and spitting, but I've got a tough hide and I don't mind if you're a little temperamental. Don't worry about Coral. What do you know about her, anyway?"

"She came to my apartment," Sallie confessed, "to warn me that you weren't serious, that you always came back to her." She tried to squirm away from his boldly exploring fingers and found instead that the friction of her skin against his made her catch her breath in longing.

He swore beneath his breath. "Women," he growled, "are the most vicious creatures on earth. Don't believe her, baby, Coral doesn't have any hold on me. I do what I want to do with whomever I choose—and right now I choose my wife."

"It isn't that easy," she insisted. "Please, Rhy, let me go. I can't make you understand when you're holding me like this—"

"Then I'll keep holding you," he interrupted. "The bottom line is this, you're mine and you'll stay mine. I can't let you go and I hope you're not in love with that photographer of yours because if you are I think I'll kill him!"

White faced, Sallie stared at him, at his suddenly narrowed eyes and clenched jaw. He reacted on a purely primitive basis to the thought of another man touching her, and abruptly she knew that it had been stupid to let him think she was involved with Chris. Not only was that a challenge to Rhy's virile domination, it wasn't fair to Chris to use him as a shield. Rhy was dangerous, he could hurt Chris and it would be her fault.

On the other hand, it went completely against her grain to let Rhy have everything his way, especially after last night. He'd certainly had everything his way then; except for that one feeble protest she'd made she hadn't attempted to ward him off at all. Even that lone effort hardly counted, because she hadn't tried to fight him off; she'd only said "no" and of course it had been a waste of breath for all the attention Rhy had paid to it.

Nor did she feel free to tell him anything about Chris. Chris's calm, lazy manner went hand in glove with such a strong sense of inner privacy that she was still surprised that he'd confided in her, and she refused to betray that confidence just to pander to Rhy's ego.

She still hadn't said anything, and suddenly Rhy's patience snapped. His hands tightened on her and he rolled, taking her with him and pinning her firmly beneath him. "Maybe you need to be shown again just who you belong to," he said violently, his mouth hard, his eyes glittering with an anger that wasn't quite anger.

Sallie's heart jolted as she felt his muscular legs parting hers, and she knew that he was going to make love to her again. Already she was drowning in the warmth that flooded her, and her heartbeat settled into a rapid pounding. But even as she slid her arms around his neck she heard herself insisting steadily, stubbornly, "I belong to myself. No one else."

"You're *mine*, Sallie! Damn you, you're *mine!*"

With his violently muttered words echoing in her ears she gave herself up to this overwhelming possession and even though her mind protested her senses were too enthralled by the delights he offered to let her argue with his blindly possessive instinct. She loved him, loved him so much that after those seven long, lonely years without his touch, now that he'd overcome her resistance and made love to her again, she wanted nothing more than to revel in the intimacy of their closeness. He couldn't give her love, but he could give her this, and it was as much of himself as he would ever give any woman. She clung to his broad shoulders and matched his fiery demands with her own, and when he finally moved from her to collapse on his back they were both satisfied and trembling with exhaustion. Unable to stand the space in the bed that separated them Sallie slid across to him and curled up against his chest, her lips pressing against his throat. As suddenly as cutting off a light she was asleep, her hands clinging to him even in sleep, as if she couldn't bear to let him go.

Awakening from her doze, Sallie stirred, opened her eyes and raised her head to find Rhy just awakening, too, his eyes still sleepy. Memories of the many mornings years ago when they'd made love and gone back to sleep made her feel eerily as if those intervening years had never been. His hand smoothed her hair back from her face, then slid around to clasp her slender neck with those strong lean fingers. "You never did tell me," he whispered. "Are you in love with him?"

She closed her eyes in resignation. He had the determination of a bulldog. But what could she tell him? Would he believe her or even understand if she told him that the way she loved Chris wasn't romantic or even sexual? The fingers clasping her neck tightened warningly and she opened her eyes. "Chris is none of your business," she said finally, tilting her chin at the grim temper that hardened his mouth. "But I haven't slept with him, so make of that what you like."

Silence followed that challenge and confession for several minutes, and when she summoned the nerve to look directly at him again she was jolted by the look of raw desire on his face. "Don't . . . don't look at me like that," she whispered, lowering her eyes again.

"I want you," he said hoarsely. "I'm going to have you. I'm glad that you don't have a lover now because I don't want any complications to stand in my way."

Wearily she shook her head. "No, you still don't understand. Just because I'm not sleeping with anyone doesn't mean that I want to take up our marriage again. For the record, I've never slept with anyone but you, but I just don't want to live with you. I don't think it'll work. Don't you see?" she pleaded. "I need my job the way you needed yours when we were first married. I can't be happy staying at home and cleaning house now, I need more, more than you're willing to give. I need my freedom.''

His face was taut as he stared at her, his eyes restless. "Don't ask me to send you on a dangerous assignment," he muttered. "I can't. If anything happened to you and I was the one responsible for your being there I couldn't live with myself. But as for the job—maybe we can work out a compromise. Let's give it a try, see how we get along together. All we ever did before was make love. We didn't get to know each other as people. We'll be here for three more days. While we're here let's just enjoy each other and worry about the future when we get back to the States. Can we manage three days together without fighting?"

"I don't know," she said cautiously. The temptation to enjoy those three days stole away her strength. She knew Rhy, knew that his idea of a compromise was to hem her in so that she had to do things his way, but there was nothing he could do while they were here. She had already taken the precaution of drawing out her savings, and once they returned to New York she knew she'd have to leave, but for now... for now why couldn't she simply enjoy being with her husband and loving him? Three days was so short a space in which to store up enough memories to last a lifetime! Why couldn't he see that they were hopelessly incompatible?

"All right," she finally agreed. "But when we get back don't expect me automatically to move in with you. I'll hold you to that compromise."

His strong mouth curved with amusement. "I never thought any differently," he said wryly, thrusting his fingers through her hair at the back of her head and pulling her down for his kiss. The kiss began casually, then gradually deepened until they were clinging together in mutual need that could only be satisfied one way.

As they dressed to attend the half-party, half-press conference that Marina was giving prior to the charity ball, Sallie was struck by how familiar it seemed, the same routine of so many years ago emerging without them having to talk about it. She used the bath first, then, while she was putting on her makeup and arranging her hair, Rhy showered and shaved. He waited until she'd put on her lipstick, then grabbed her and kissed her, smearing the color outside her lip line, chuckling to himself as she flounced back to the mirror to repair the job. How many times had he done that in the past? She couldn't remember. It was part of their marriage, and when she met his eyes in the mirror she knew that he was remembering, too, and they smiled at each other.

The gown she'd chosen was a pale rose silk, simply cut, as her lack of stature wouldn't permit anything frivolous or she looked like a doll. The color was extremely flattering to her dark blue eyes and glossy sable hair and Rhy eyed her with male appreciation as he zipped her up.

"I don't think it's safe for you to leave this room." He bent down to murmur in her ear. "Some wild sheik will steal you and take you into the desert and I'll have to start a war to get you back again."

"What? And ruin a good story?" she mocked, meeting his eyes in the mirror. "I'm certain I could escape, and just think what good reading that would make!"

"I would laugh," he said wryly, "but I know first-hand the kind of dangers you've faced, and it damned near curdles my blood. It's one thing for me to risk my hide and quite another for yours to be endangered."

"Not really," she argued, leaning forward to brush her finger under her eye and remove a tiny smudge she'd just noticed. "When we were together before, I was terrified that you'd be hurt and I nearly died when you were shot. Now I understand what sent you back to the field as soon as possible, because I became hooked on excitement, too."

"It wears off," he said, an almost weary look passing over his hard features. "The danger became almost a bore, and the thought of sleeping in the same bed for more than a few days in a row grew in attractiveness. Roots don't necessarily tie you down, baby, they can help you to grow bigger."

"That's true, if the pot's large enough so that you don't become root-bound," she pointed out and turned to face him. She was smiling but the expression in her eyes was serious and he tilted her face up to him with one long finger under her chin.

"But holding on to you is so much fun," he teased.

"Don't you ever think of anything else?" She shook her head in amusement.

"When I'm with you? Rarely." His gray eyes took on a glint of passion as he looked down at her. "Even before I knew who you were all I had to do was catch a glimpse of that sassy braid switching back and forth across your trim little rear and I wanted to chase you down in the hallways."

Sallie smiled, but inwardly she recognized that all of his words, his actions, were based on physical attraction and not on an emotional need. Rhy wanted her, there was no doubt about that, but the realization was growing in her that he was incapable of love. Perhaps it was just as well. If he loved as intensely as he desired, his love could be soul destroying.

The party was being held in another hotel as the Al Mahdi palace was being readied for the ball and Marina's husband did not want their own home opened to the public for security reasons. The circular drive in front of the hotel was choked with limousines and there was a confusing mixture of accents as Europeans and Americans mingled with the native Sakaryans. Security was tight; the doors and lower windows were posted with guards, fierce-looking Sakaryans in boots and military uniforms, with cocky little berets on their heads, watching the crowd of foreign visitors with their fierce black desert eyes. Their credentials and invitation were checked and rechecked as Sallie and Rhy moved slowly forward in the swarm of people.

But once inside they were guided smoothly into the suite being used and all outward signs of security vanished. There was soft, soothing music playing and the light tinkle of ice cubes against glass testified that many people were relaxing.

The suite was simply furnished in the Arabic way, but there were enough seats for anyone who preferred to sit instead of stand. The colors blended simply, golds and browns and whites, and Sallie discerned Marina's touch in the many plants and flowers that dotted the rooms and both cheered and soothed. She looked about for her friend but was unable to catch sight of her in the constantly moving flow of humanity.

"Why is the security so stiff outside?" she asked, leaning close to Rhy so no one else could hear her.

"Because Zain isn't a fool," Rhy growled. "A lot of people would like to see him dead. Relatives of the King who are jealous of Zain's influence, religious purists who don't like his progressive politics, terrorist left-wingers who don't need a reason, even Communists. Sakarya is an important hunk of real estate these days."

"I heard about the oil reserves," she whispered. "Are they that large?"

"Massive. If the surveys prove correct Sakarya will have reserves second only to the Saudis."

"I see," she mused. "And since the finance minister is married to an American woman his sympathies will naturally lean to the West. That makes his influence with the King doubly important. Good heavens, is it safe for Marina to live here?"

"As safe as Zain can make it, and he's a cunning man. He intends to die of old age."

She intended to ask more but a flash of bright hair caught her eye, and she turned her head to see Marina bearing down on her. Her friend was gorgeous, glowing, her lovely spring green eyes sparkling with gaiety. "Sallie!" she exclaimed, laughing, and the two hugged each other enthusiastically. "I wasn't sure you were going to make it! I couldn't believe it. Someone kept wanting to send another reporter in your place. I refused to see her, of course," she said with laughing triumph.

"Of course," agreed Sallie. "By the way, Marina, let me introduce my publisher, Rhydon Baines. He's the one who tried to foul things up for us."

"You're kidding!" Marina smiled up at Rhy and gave him her hand. "Didn't you know Sallie and I are old friends?"

"Not until after the fireworks," he said wryly. "I soon found out. Is Zain here? It's been a long time since I've seen him."

Recognition lit Marina's eyes. "You're *that* Rhy Baines? Yes, he's here somewhere." She turned her head to locate her husband, peering around groups of people. "Here he comes now."

Zain ibn Rashid was a lean, pantherish man with a darkly aquiline face and a rather cruel smile, but he wore his exquisitely tailored suit as casually as an American teenager would wear jeans. Sensuality curled his upper lip and hooded his piercing black eyes, and with a shock Sallie realized that she'd only met one other man who exuded that aura of raw sexuality, Rhy. It was ironic but rather inevitable that she and Marina had married the same type of man, both untamed and unlikely ever to be tamed.

"Rhy!" Zain had transferred his gaze from his wife to glance casually at the couple with her and now his black eyes opened with recognition and he extended his hand. "I'd heard you were going to interview the King, then that the plans were changed. Are you going to do the interview after all?"

"No, someone else will do that. I'm here on a different matter entirely," Rhy said in a wry tone, nodding his head to indicate Sallie. "I'm here as a bodyguard for the reporter from *World in Review*. Sallie, let me introduce Zain Abdul ibn Rashid, the minister of finance—"

"And my husband," Marina broke in impishly. "Zain, Sallie is my friend I've been telling you about." Then she looked at Rhy. "What do you mean, bodyguard? I thought you were the publisher of the magazine?"

"I am," he admitted, unperturbed. "I'm also her husband."

Irrepressible Marina squealed and hugged Sallie again. "You're married! When did this happen? Why didn't you write me?"

"I haven't had time," Sallie blurted without thinking while she shot Rhy a glance that promised revenge. He merely smiled at her, well satisfied with his announcement.

Zain was grinning openly. "So you finally got caught. We'll have to celebrate, but when I don't know. Marina has thrown the country into an uproar. I'll be glad when this is over." He gave his wife a look that held for several seconds before he jerked his eyes away, but Sallie had seen his expression and she heaved an inward sigh of relief. He'd looked at Marina with absorbing tenderness before pulling his sardonic mask back in place. He really loved Marina; he hadn't chosen her simply for her golden beauty.

"I can't stay any longer, I have to circulate." Marina sighed, putting her hand on Zain's arm. "Sallie, I promise that after the ball we'll curl up and talk our heads off."

Sallie nodded. "I'll see you then," she said as Marina left to attend to the other guests, with Zain a watchful escort.

"She's beautiful," Rhy commented.

"Yes." She glanced at him from under her lashes. "Even more beautiful than Coral."

"Am I supposed to argue with that?" he drawled.

She shrugged and didn't answer. Instead she questioned, "How long have you known Zain?"

"Several years," he said noncommittally.

"How did you meet him?"

"What is this, an interview?" he parried, taking her arm and steering her to the side. He signaled a waiter who came over with a tray of glasses. Rhy took two glasses of champagne and gave one to Sallie.

"Why aren't you answering me?" she persisted, and at last he gave her an exasperated look.

"Because, baby, I wouldn't like my answers to be overheard, and neither would Zain. Now be a good girl, and stop being so nosy."

She glared at him and turned her back, walking slowly among the ebb and flow of people as she sipped from her glass. Nosy! Asking questions was her job and he knew it. But he was the most contrary man she'd ever met, she thought idly, tracing her finger along the rim of a jade vase. Contrary and arrogant, he didn't know what it meant to be thwarted in anything he wanted.

"Stop sulking and start taking notes," he whispered in her ear. "Notice who's here and who isn't."

"I don't need you to tell me how to do my job," she flared, walking away from him again.

"No, what you need is a good spanking," he murmured, his long legs and greater strength making it easy for him to stay even with her in the press of people.

Perhaps he had hoped to get a rise out of her with that ridiculous statement, but she ignored him and continued her wandering progress through the suite.

She rarely took notes at a function like this, having learned that it made people self-conscious. One of her assets was that she had an excellent memory and she used it, identifying the European blue bloods and financial giants. Social events weren't really her field, but she was able to put a name and a country to the important people and most of the not-so-important ones, as well.

Rhy caught her arm and leaned down to whisper, "There's the Deputy Secretary of State to your right. And the French foreign minister beside him."

"I know," Sallie said smugly, having already spotted the two men. "But I haven't seen a representative of a Communist nation, so I suppose Zain's influence is making itself felt."

Just then a tall, thin, distinguished gentleman with gray hair and kindly blue eyes approached them and extended his hand. "Mr. Baines," he greeted Rhy cordially in a clipped British public school accent. "Nice to see you again."

"It's a pleasure to meet you again, Mr. Ambassador," Rhy replied, taking the other man's hand. "Sallie, I'd like to introduce you to Sir Alexander Wilson-Hume, Great Britain's ambassador to Sakarya. Mr. Ambassador, my wife, Sallie."

The pale blue eyes lit as the ambassador took Sallie's hand and gently lifted it to his lips with old-world courtesy. "My pleasure entirely." He smiled as Sallie murmured a conventional greeting. "Have you been married long, Mrs. Baines?"

An impish smile curved her lips. "Eight years, Mr. Ambassador."

"My word! Eight years!" He gave her a startled glance and abruptly she wondered if he'd had reason to assume that Rhy wasn't married when he'd known him before. But if that was the case the ambassador covered his confusion with perfect poise and carried on without a hitch. "You hardly look old enough to have been married a year."

"That's true," Rhy agreed smoothly. "She's aged well."

The ambassador gave him a rather startled glance, but Sallie merely smiled at Rhy's impudence despite the hollow ache that had bloomed inside her at the thought of Rhy's blatant infidelities. She'd just have to get over that, she told herself firmly. Only a naive fool would expect a man like Rhy to be faithful; he was far too physical, and far too attractive!

It was several hours later, when they were at last in a taxi returning to their own hotel, that Sallie commented evenly, "Poor man, the ambassador covered up for you well, didn't he? But now he considers you a philanderer."

"I'd hoped you wouldn't notice," Rhy replied wryly, "but you don't miss much, do you? But don't paint me blacker than I am, Sallie. You said you never thought I'd live like a monk, but I very nearly did. I've had a lot of social dates that ended when I took the lady home, nothing more."

"You're lying," she stated without expression. "I suppose you expect me to believe that Coral Williams is just a friend?"

"She's not my enemy," he said, his mouth twitching in amusement. She didn't believe him when he continued. "I wanted to make you think she was my mistress to make you jealous, but I guess it didn't work."

She began to laugh in disbelief. She'd never heard such a ridiculous tale before in her life. Rhy was a sensual animal, his passions never far from the surface, and easily aroused. She'd have to be a fool to believe he'd been faithful to her during the seven years they'd been separated. She didn't even believe he'd been faithful to her while they'd been together! "Sorry." She laughed. "Try a tale that's more plausible. Besides, it doesn't matter."

He drew in his breath in a hiss, and glancing at him she saw the flare of anger in his eyes. "I'll make it matter," he promised her grimly. Or was it a threat?

She knew that he intended to make love to her as soon as they were in their hotel room in an attempt to tear down her convictions, and she eyed him warily. She'd agreed to spend the three days with him and she'd known that they would be sleeping together, but she intended to limit their lovemaking to the nights. After all, his desire was familiar to her, even after all these years. What she wanted to do was talk to him, learn about him, get to know him in the way she'd never known him before. He was her husband, but he was still a stranger to her. Sadly she realized that even though she planned on leaving when they returned to New York she was still searching for some way to believe that they could be happy together even when she knew the search was futile.

They had just entered the hotel room, and Rhy was shrugging out of his formal jacket when the phone rang. With an impatient curse he snatched it up and barked, "Yes?"

Sallie watched him as he listened, saw the frown that darkened his brow. "I'll be right down," he said, and hung up, then pulled his jacket back on.

"Who was that?" she asked.

"The desk. There's a message for me. I'll be right back."

After he'd gone she undressed and hung away her gown, then put on a lightweight white blouson dress, all the while mulling over what he'd said. A message for him? Why hadn't they given it to him over the phone or, better yet, when they'd walked through the lobby not five minutes before? It didn't sound plausible, and without hesitation she left the room and made for the elevators. She made her living by being curious, after all.

But she was more than curious, she was cautious. She left the elevator at the second floor and walked down the stairs the rest of the way. Her cautiousness was rewarded. She opened the door at the bottom of the stairs and looked out to see her husband standing with his arm around Coral Williams, who was staring up at him with tearstained eyes. Sallie couldn't hear what they were saying, but Rhy went with Coral to the elevators and the doors slid shut behind them.

Her lips pressed firmly together, Sallie returned to their hotel room and swiftly gathered her clothing. So much for his tale of being faithful! It had to be more than a casual relationship for Coral to follow him to Sakarya. And she wasn't going to wait for him to listen to any more of his lies!

She had to act swiftly; she had no way of knowing how long he would stay with Coral. She scribbled a note, not paying attention to what she was writing, but it was something to the effect of sorry, she just wasn't interested. Then she picked up her suitcase and purse and left, once again taking the stairs.

Finding a taxi was easy, a fleet of them was waiting outside the hotel; her problem now was finding a place to stay. She was aware that hotels were few and far between in Khalidia. In French she explained to the driver that she wished to go to another hotel but not one that was well-known. He obliged, and when Sallie saw it she understood why it wasn't well-known; it looked as if the French Foreign Legion should come swarming over the walls. It was small and old and simple, and the fiercely mustachioed man who seemed to be in charge looked her over thoroughly before saying something in his own language to the taxi driver.

"He says there is a room, if you wish it, but it is not of the finest," the driver translated. "Also you must pay in advance and you must stay in your room as you are not veiled and your man is not with you."

"That seems fair," Sallie replied. To stay in the room was just what the doctor ordered; it would insure that Rhy couldn't find her. "But what shall I do for food?"

The Sakaryan's dark eyes slid over her, and then he revealed that he spoke some French by informing her rustily that his wife would bring food to her.

Delighted that she'd be able to communicate Sallie thanked him and beamed at him, her big eyes sparkling. When the driver had left Sallie lifted her suitcase and waited expectantly for her host to lead her way to her room. Instead he glared down at her fiercely for a moment, then leaned down and took the suitcase from her hand. "You are too small," he growled. "My wife will feed you."

Then he took her up the narrow stairs to her room and left her there, and Sallie examined what was to be her sleeping quarters for the next two nights. The room was spotless but contained only a single bed and a washstand on which stood a blue urn of water and a washbasin. But the bed was covered with an exotic spread and was strewn with cushions, and the mattress was comfortable, so she was satisfied.

The proprietor's wife brought up a tray loaded with cheese, bread, orange juice and coffee. She looked Sallie over from head to toe, her expression shocked at the sight of Sallie's slim legs, but she gave a timid smile in response to Sallie's grin.

After eating, Sallie took off her dress and shoes; if she was to be confined in this small room for forty-eight hours she might as well be comfortable. Digging in her suitcase she produced the long T-shirt that she had packed and pulled it on; wearing only that and her panties she was as cool as she could get and still have any clothes on. Then she unpacked her clothing and hung everything up to air.

With nothing else to do she lay down on the bed and tried to lose herself in one of the paperback books she'd brought, but the heat was becoming oppressive and she thought with longing of the air-conditioned comfort of the Hotel Khalidia. Flopping onto her back she raised the book to fan herself, and only then did she notice the old-fashioned paddle fan on the ceiling. "Shades of *Casablanca!*" she cried in delight, jumping up and looking about for the switch. She wouldn't even have sworn that the hotel was wired for electricity, but there was a switch on the wall, and when she flipped it the fan creaked into motion. The gentle movement of air against her skin relieved the sensation of smothering, and she fell back on the bed.

She tried again to read her book, but thoughts of Rhy kept breaking into her concentration, and suddenly a raw sob burst from her throat. Amazed at her tears and yet helpless to stop them, she bowed her head onto the bed and wept until her chest hurt and her eyes were swollen. Crying for Rhy? She'd sworn seven years ago that he'd never make her cry again, and she had thought she was over all her illusions about him, but seeing him with his arm around Coral had hit her like a sledgehammer. Was she always going to be a fool over the man? What was the old saying? "I have cried for these things once already," or something to that effect, yet here she was crying for them again. And it was a waste of time.

She should be glad that she'd seen Coral before she'd allowed Rhy to make a complete fool of her. It was her stupid weakness for him that allowed her, even knowing that she was stupid, still to respond to his lovemaking—crave his lovemaking, if she was honest with herself. And subconsciously she'd been hoping that somehow things would work out between them. She might as well face the truth once and for all: the reasons Rhy wanted her back were not emotional ones; they were all physical. Sex between them was good. It was more than good. They were a matched pair with their needs, their instincts and responses, each knowing just how to drive the other wild. And it wasn't anything they thought about; it was inborn in both of them, whatever it was that made each of them so physically attractive to the other.

Having known his lovemaking, hadn't she refused all other men because she'd known that they couldn't compare with what she'd had with Rhy? She couldn't see Rhy refusing women like that; his sexual appetites were too urgent and strong, but there was no doubt that he had a weakness for her. But sex just wasn't enough for her! She loved him and she wanted that love to be returned. They couldn't spend their lives together in bed; there had to be something else.

With fierce determination she dried her tears and looked about for something to do. Reading couldn't help and she wished that she had brought her manuscript with her. But even if it wasn't here she could write in longhand, couldn't she, and type it up when she returned home? She knew that she could lose herself in writing, push the pain inside her away.

She never went anywhere without several pads tucked into her bag so she dug one out and sat down on the bed with it balanced on her knee, as there was nothing to use for a desk. Grimly she made herself recall where she'd left off, and after a few minutes the writing became easier. So what if Rhy had let her down again? She still had herself, her newly discovered talent and her integrity. She had learned how to live without Rhy, and she'd been a fool to have stayed with the magazine once she had learned he'd bought it. She was vulnerable to him, she always had been, but she knew that she didn't dare let him resume the prominent position that he'd once held in her life. It had nearly destroyed her, that mad need for his touch, his smile, his presence.

But what if she had a baby? The thought came out of nowhere and she dropped her pen, her hand straying over her flat stomach, and she wondered. Thinking back, counting, she realized that it was possible, even likely. But there was a difference now: she wouldn't be terrified at being on her own. She would gladly welcome a chance to have her child all to herself. Part of her longed for a baby, ached to hold a small wriggling body in her arms. She'd never been able to hold her son; they had taken him away immediately and she'd had only a glimpse of his blue little face. Another baby...another son. Suddenly she hoped it was so with a fierce, wild yearning. Perhaps she couldn't have Rhy, but she could have his baby, and she could give to her child the love that Rhy didn't want.

Chapter Eight

On the morning of the charity ball Sallie was a mass of nerves, partly a result of being shut up in that tiny room for two days and partly because she so dreaded facing Rhy again. She knew as well as she knew the color of her eyes that he hadn't left the city; he was waiting for her to surface at the ball. He would be furious, and that was an understatement.

But she dressed in the lavender silk dress that she'd chosen for the ball and noticed that it darkened her eyes to violet. A touch of mauve eyeshadow made her eyes pools of mystery and she underlined the air of sophistication by pulling her hair back from her face in a severe coil that was secured by three tiny amethyst butterflies.

It was almost time for her taxi, so she picked up her suitcase, since she would not be coming back there after the ball, and carefully made her way down the narrow stairs, not wanting to turn her ankles in her high heels. The Sakaryan proprietor was seated just to the right of the stairs, and he got to his feet as she descended. His gaze went over her thoroughly, and she sensed the tension of his powerful muscles. She had the uncomfortable feeling that this Sakaryan would like to start a harem, with her as his first concubine!

But he said, in his rough French, "It is dangerous for you to be in this part of the city alone. I will walk with you to the taxi, yes?"

"Yes, thank you," she said gravely, and noticed that he didn't offer to carry the suitcase for her this time, but she was grateful for his escort even for the short distance to the taxi waiting outside. Her driver grinned and got out to open the door as they approached.

At the palace gates she had to leave the taxi as the driver wasn't cleared to enter the palace grounds. Her name was checked off on the list of guests and a hawk-faced guard escorted her to the palace and even stored her suitcase in a small cupboard before taking her to the enormous chamber that had been decorated for the ball.

Though she was early there were already a fair number of people standing about, the women dressed like so many butterflies, and the abundance of jewels made her eyebrows arch. To her delight there were also a number of Muslim guests, and she was certain that not all of the dark men, some wearing their native headdress and some in European clothing, were Sakaryan; probably Rhy could put a name to most of them. And there were a few Muslim women, too, well dressed, quiet, looking about with their huge, liquid dark eyes. She would have loved to talk to them, ask about their lives, but she had the feeling that her nosiness wouldn't be very well received.

Suddenly Sallie felt a tingle along the left side of her face, and she lifted a hand to touch her cheek. Then she knew, and she turned her head slightly to look straight into Rhy's furious gaze. His eyes were like flint, his jaw carved out of granite. Sallie tilted her chin and gave him back as good as she got as he strode toward her with suppressed savagery in every line of his muscular body.

She stood her ground, and when he reached her he encircled her slim waist with his hard fingers, a grip that didn't hurt but which she knew she couldn't break. A voice gravelly with temper growled, "You need to be shown who's boss, baby, and I'm just the man to do it. Where the *hell* have you been?"

"At another hotel," she informed him casually. "I told you from the beginning that I didn't want to resume our marriage, and I meant it."

"You agreed to give it a three-day trial," he reminded her grimly.

"So I did. I'd have agreed to rob a bank if it would have kept you from watching me. So what?" She raised her head and looked him straight in the eye. "I lied to you and you lied to me. We're even."

"How did I lie to you?" he snapped, his nostrils flaring in rage that he had to control because they were in public.

"About Coral." She gave him a wintry smile. "You don't seem to realize that I don't mind if you had other women—I really don't *care*—" that was a lie if she'd ever told one "—but I do object to people lying to me. So you've been a virtual monk, have you? Am I to believe that Coral followed you all the way to Sakarya with tears in her beautiful eyes on the basis of a platonic relationship?"

"I don't know how you found out about Coral—" he began impatiently, but she interrupted.

"I followed you. I have a nosy nature. It's part of being a reporter. So, my dear husband, I saw you comfort your mistress and take her to her room, and you didn't leave immediately or you would have caught *me* leaving!"

"It's your fault that I took her to her room," he snarled, his fingers tightening on her wrist. "I didn't ask her to follow me and I didn't lie to you. She isn't and never has been my mistress. But there she was, and she was crying, and I wondered if you'd been right when you said she was in love with me. I've never thought she was, she went out with other men, and I dated other women, but there was the possibility that you'd seen something I'd missed. I thought I owed her an explanation, so I took her to her room and told her the truth about us. Fifteen minutes later I went back to our room and found only that damned note of yours! I could break your neck, Sallie. I've been half out of my mind worrying about you!''

"I've told you I can take care of myself," she muttered, wondering if she could believe this or not. But she didn't dare believe him! How could she? She knew him too well, knew the strength of his sexual appetite.

Further conversation was prevented at that point by the entrance of the King of Sakarya, His Royal Highness Abu Haroun al Mahdi. Everyone bowed and the women curtsied, including the Americans in the group, and the King looked pleased. He lacked the stature of many Sakaryans, but five hundred years of rule were evident in his proud carriage and straightforward gaze. He greeted his guests first in perfect English, then in French, and finally in the Arabic tongue.

Sallie strained up on her toes for a better look at him, and for a moment her eyes were solidly locked with those of the monarch. After a second's hesitation he gave her a nod and a slow, faintly shy smile which she returned with her own warm, friendly smile; then they were blocked from view by a group of people moving closer to him.

"You've made a hit," Rhy observed with narrowed eyes.

"All I did was smile at him," she defended crossly, for it seemed as if he was accusing her of something.

"Your smile is an open invitation, baby," he drawled.

He was going to be impossible; he would make the day as difficult for her as he could. "Isn't it time for the fashion show to begin?" she said, grateful for anything that would relieve her of his undivided attention.

"In half an hour," he replied, drawing her with him to the room where the fashion show would take place. Some of the top designers of the world had put together the show for Marina and already the chairs that had been placed about the runway were half filled. Exquisitely gowned women laughed and chattered while their suave escorts looked on with veiled interest.

A thought struck Sallie and she muttered to Rhy, "I suppose Coral is modeling?"

"Of course," he affirmed, his voice hard.

"Then we might as well find seats," she sniped. "I don't suppose wild horses could drag you away."

His fingers bit painfully into her arm. "Shut up," he snarled. "My God, can't you just shut up?" His head snapped around and before she could protest he was marching her firmly out of the room. He barked a question at a guard who saluted smartly, for some reason, and led them down a passageway to a small room. Rhy bodily pushed her into the room and closed the door behind them.

Hoping to divert him from the black rage she could see in his face Sallie said hastily, "What room is this?"

while she looked around the small chamber as if she was vastly interested.

"I don't care," Rhy replied, his voice so rough that the words were barely intelligible, and then he advanced on her with dark purpose evident in his face. Sallie backed away in alarm but had taken only a few steps when he caught her.

He didn't say anything else; he simply pulled her to him and covered her mouth with his and kissed her with such devouring hunger that she forgot to struggle. It would have been useless in any case; she was no match for his strength and he held her so closely that their bodies were pressed together from shoulder to knee. Blood began to drum in her ears and she sank against him, held up only by his arms.

Long minutes later he lifted his mouth and surveyed her flushed, love-drugged face. "Don't talk to me about other women," he ordered in a low tone, his uneven breath caressing her lips. "No other woman can excite me like you do, even when you're not trying to, you little witch. I want you now," he finished on a groan, bending his head to brush her lips with his.

"That—that's impossible," she whispered, but her protest was only a token one. The sensual fire that burned in him burned in her, also, and if he had persisted she wouldn't have been capable of resisting. As it was he retained some sense of their location and put her away from him with shaking hands.

"I know, dammit." He sighed. "I suppose we'd better go back if you want to see the fashion show—

and not another word about Coral," he warned darkly.

Her fingers trembling, she repaired the damage he'd done to her lipstick and offered him a tissue to wipe the color from his mouth. He did so, smiling a little at the smear of color that came off on the tissue.

"What did you say to the guard?" she finally asked, obeying a need to make nonvital conversation.

"I told him you were feeling faint," he replied. "And you did look pale."

"Do I now?" she wondered aloud, touching her cheeks.

"No. You look kissed," he drawled.

The blood was still rushing through her body in yearning when they took their seats for the fashion show, and the parade of models barely registered on her consciousness. She was too aware of Rhy's tall body beside her, so close that she could feel the warmth of him, smell the unique muskiness of his body. Her heart pounded heavily in her chest. Only Coral made any impression on her, her eyes fastened on Rhy as if drawn to him, the pouty, sensuous smile on her perfect mouth meant for him alone. Glancing sideways at Rhy, Sallie saw that his expression remained closed except for a slight tightening of his jaw that spoke volumes to her, and she looked back at Coral with nausea boiling in her stomach.

The program was full, every minute ordered. After the fashion show there was a thousand-dollar-a-plate dinner, with all of the proceeds going to charity. Then dancing, then entertainment by a top American singer. Sallie lived through the hours feeling as if she was walking underwater. Rhy was with her every minute, but she couldn't forget the fleeting expression on his face when he'd seen Coral.

Why was she allowing him to torment her like this? She had no illusions about him, and she had already determined her own course of action. When they returned to New York she would leave, it was as simple as that. But for some reason she couldn't shake her deep sense of misery, and as a result she drank more champagne than she meant to, realizing that fact only when the room swirled mistily around her and she clutched at Rhy's arm.

"That's enough," he said gently, taking the glass from her fingers and setting it down. "I think you could stand something to eat, a slice of cake maybe. Come on."

With tender concern he made certain she ate, watching her closely all the while. When she felt better she smiled thankfully at him. "How much longer before the interview?" she murmured.

"Not much longer, honey," he comforted, as if sensing her unhappiness.

But at last it was over with and Sallie and Marina were alone in a private chamber the King had donated for their use. "He's really a dear," Marina explained. "I think he's shy, but he tries so hard to disguise it. And of course he was brought up to disregard women in every way but the physical, and he can't quite become used to meeting them socially despite his English education."

"Did your husband go to the same school?" Sallie asked, thinking that Zain didn't seem to have any problem with women.

"No, and his attitude could bear some improvement, too," Marina said with wry amusement. "Listen, he kept a harem until we were engaged. I made him give them all up before I would agree to marry him!" she explained smugly.

Sallie choked on her laughter and gasped. "A harem? You're kidding! Do they still have those things?"

"Of course, why do you think the royal families have so many princes? Muslim religion permits three wives and as many concubines as a man can support, and Zain most definitely had his selection of concubines to occupy his nights!"

"What did you say to him to make him give them up?"

"I gave him a choice, he could have me or he could have other women, but I made it plain that I had no intention of sharing him. He didn't like the idea of giving up his harem, but he finally realized that my ignorant American mind just couldn't accept it."

Their eyes met and they went off into gales of laughter, and of course that was the moment when they were interrupted by Rhy and Zain. "I thought this was a serious interview," Rhy commented, strolling forward to drop his long length beside Sallie.

"And I thought it was a private one," she retorted.

Zain's strong mouth quirked as he stretched his long frame out close to Marina. "We couldn't resist," he explained. "I introduced Rhy to His Majesty," he said, flexing his broad shoulders as if he was weary, and he chuckled at the memory. "I think I made some diplomats jealous, especially when they had a long chat in voices too low to carry!"

"The State Department will probably try to debrief me," Rhy added.

A memory clicked in Sallie's mind, and she said casually to Zain, "How did you meet Rhy?"

"He saved my life," Zain replied promptly, but no explanation followed and Sallie's eyebrows arched.

"You don't need to know," Rhy teased. "We were both where we weren't supposed to be and we barely got out alive. Let it rest, baby. Tell us how you and Marina met, instead."

"Oh, that's simple enough." Marina shrugged. "We met in college. There's nothing unusual in that. Now, why don't you two run along? How can Sallie and I talk with witnesses present?"

Both men laughed, but neither made a move to leave, so they had to be included in the conversation. To be truthful, it was impossible to exclude them. Rhy wasn't there for an interview, but he was still a reporter and gradually he got one anyway. Despite her exasperation Sallie could only admire the way he posed his questions to Zain. Some were blunt, posed point-blank; others he merely hinted at, letting Zain evade the question or answer it as he wished. In response to that consideration Zain was open with his answers, and Sallie knew that she was listening to potential dynamite. He told Rhy things that perhaps even foreign heads of state hadn't been told, and he seemed to have perfect confidence that Rhy would know what he could report and what he should forget.

Slowly Sallie began to understand the razor-sharp brain of the man who handled the finances of a booming economy and was slowly easing his country into the twentieth century. He was an adventurer, but he was also a patriot. Perhaps that was why the King had such great confidence in his young minister of finance, why he was allowing Sakaryan policies to be shaped along Western lines.

The role that Marina played in those policies wasn't small, she realized. As Zain had vast influence with the King, so Marina had vast influence with Zain. She didn't know if he would admit it; a man who had kept a harem until fairly recently wasn't likely to admit even to himself that his wife was a major factor in the direction his politics had taken. Nor would the King be likely to be happy if told that Marina was the indirect influence behind his throne. Yet the smiling, beautiful young woman, so obviously in love with her husband, was playing a powerful role in a scenario that could affect the entire world through its effect of Sakaryan oil.

At last the conversation became more general and Marina asked if perhaps Sallie would be free to visit later on in the year. Sallie had opened her mouth to accept when Rhy broke in before she could say a word. "I'm set to be filming a documentary in Europe late this fall and early winter," he said, "and Sallie will be with me. I don't know yet how the schedule will be, but I'll let you know."

"Do," urged Marina. "We see each other so little now. At least when I lived in New York we managed to catch each other in town once every month or so."

Sallie didn't comment, but privately she thought that Rhy was taking a lot for granted. Was he in for a surprise when she walked out of his life and disappeared forever!

It was late when they left the palace, and as they just had time to catch their flight Zain had arranged for an escort to the airport. Sallie and Rhy rode in Zain's personal limousine, and their luggage was checked and they were waved on board without pause.

Rhy had been ominously silent during the entire ride, and he was still not speaking when they buckled themselves into their seats. That suited her fine; she was tired and she didn't feel like arguing with him. Somehow she always came off second best when they fought. She was too impulsive, too reckless, unable to control her temper, whereas Rhy coolly plotted each move in advance.

When they were airborne the stewardesses began distributing the small airline pillows and blankets to those passengers who desired them, and because it was so late Sallie decided she would try to sleep and accepted them, then tilted her seat back. "I'm tired," she told Rhy's grim profile. "Good night."

He turned his head and his hard eyes burned her. Then he let his seat back, too, and slid his arm under her head, pulling her over to rest on his shoulder. "I've spent two hellish nights wondering where you were," he growled against her temple while he spread the blanket over her. "You'll sleep where you belong." Then he tilted her head back and his hard mouth closed on hers, claiming her lips in a possessive kiss that lasted long enough for him to be aware of her response. Then he drew back and resettled her head against his shoulder, and she was glad of the chance to hide her burning face. Why did she have to be so weak and foolish? Why couldn't she control her response to him?

After that kiss she was sure she wouldn't be able to sleep, but somehow she fell asleep immediately and woke only once during the long flight when she shifted and Rhy pulled the blanket up over her again. Opening her eyes in the dim cabin she looked up at him and whispered, "Can't you sleep?"

"I've been asleep," he murmured. "I was just wishing that we were alone." He pulled her close and kissed her again, leaving her in no doubt as to just why he wished they were alone. His kisses lingered and became hungry, pressing again and again to her mouth, until at last he muttered a frustrated curse and leaned his head back. "I can wait," he growled. "Barely."

Sallie lay against his shoulder and bit her lips to keep from whispering the words of love that sprang to her tongue. Tears burned her eyes. She loved him! It was so painful that she thought she'd scream. She loved him, but she couldn't trust him with her love.

They changed flights in Paris again and because the days they had spent in Sakarya hadn't been exactly restful jet lag hit both of them hard. Sallie had a splitting headache when they finally landed at JFK and from the taut, weary look on Rhy's face he didn't feel much better. If he had started an argument then she would have become hysterical, but instead he dropped her at her apartment and left without even kissing her.

Contrarily, that made her want to cry, and she lugged her suitcase up to her apartment and savagely emptied it. After taking a swift shower she fell on the bed and found to her fury that sleep eluded her. She remembered the sleepy sensuousness of his kisses during the flight, how comfortable she had been cuddled against his shoulder, the security of his arms. She burst into angry, aching tears and eventually cried herself to sleep.

But when she awoke the next morning her mind was clear. Rhy was driving her crazy, and if she didn't leave now, as she had planned, he would eventually wear her down. She would go to work today, type up the interview she had gotten with Marina and quietly turn in her notice to Greg. Then she would come back home, close up the apartment, pack her clothing and get on a bus going anywhere.

She dressed and took the bus to work, arriving a little late due to an accident that caused a traffic jam. When she entered the noisy newsroom the clatter dropped to almost silence, and it seemed to her that everyone turned to stare at her. A blush rose to her cheeks without her knowing why, and she hurried to her little cubicle. Brom was there, busy at his typewriter, but when she sat down and pulled the cover off of her own typewriter he stopped what he was doing and swiveled in his chair to look at her.

"What's wrong?" Sallie demanded, half laughing. "Do I have something on my face?"

In answer Brom leaned over and turned her wooden nameplate to face her. Aghast, Sallie stared at it. It was a new nameplate. And instead of SALLIE JEROME it blatantly declared for all the world to see, SALLIE BAINES. She collapsed in her chair and stared at it as if it would bite her.

"Congratulations," Brom offered. "That must've been some trip."

She couldn't think of anything to say; she just continued to stare at the nameplate. Evidently it had only appeared that morning, and she wondered at Rhy's motive. Uneasily she sensed that he was drawing the net tighter about her and that perhaps she had waited too long to make her break. But there was no help for it now, and her professional integrity wouldn't permit her to leave without finishing the interview with Marina.

"Well?" Brom prompted. "Is it true?"

"That we're married?" she replied crisply. "It's true enough, for what you want to make of it."

"And just what does that mean, Madam Sphinx?"

"It means that a wedding does not a marriage make," she mocked. "Don't take this too seriously."

"Listen, you can't be half-married, or casually married. Either you are or you aren't," he said in exasperation.

"It's a long story," she evaded, and was saved from further questioning when the phone rang. With a smothered sigh of relief she snatched it up. "Sallie Jerome."

"Wrong," Greg growled in her ear. "Sallie *Baines*. Your closet husband has gone public and it's a load off my mind. You had me in a tough spot if he'd found out I knew about you. But it's all over now and it's all between the two of you."

"What do you mean?" she asked warily, wondering if Rhy had done something else to hem her in that she hadn't yet heard of.

"Just that, doll. As far as I'm concerned you're not one of my best reporters now, you're his wife."

In blind anger Sallie forgot that she'd been planning on turning in her notice anyway and she hissed between her teeth, "Do you mean you won't give me any more assignments?"

"That's exactly what I mean. Take it up directly with him. For crying out loud, he's your husband and from what I can see he's more than willing to try a reconciliation."

"I don't want a reconciliation," she said, reining in her temper and keeping her tone low so Brom couldn't overhear. "But a reference will do just fine. Will you give me one?"

"I can't, not now that he's made it common knowledge that you're his wife. He's my boss, too," Greg explained dryly. "And he's made it clear that anything concerning you is to be okayed by him personally."

"Has he?" she demanded furiously as her anger broke out of control. "I'll have to see about that, won't I?" She slammed the phone down and glared at it, then turned her burning gaze on Brom, who threw his hands up in mock surrender and ostentatiously turned back to his typewriter.

She expected to be summoned to Rhy's office at any moment, and she couldn't decide if she wanted to see him or not. It would be an exquisite relief to unleash her temper and scream at him, but she knew that Rhy would also take advantage of her lack of control and would probably provoke her into revealing all her plans. The best thing she could do was to complete her report and leave. She knew her weaknesses, and the two worst ones were her temper and Rhy. The sensible thing to do was not to allow either of them to gain the upper hand.

She tried, but concentrating had seldom been more difficult. Her mind raced, going over her packing, the steps she had to take to close up her apartment, where she might go, and in the middle of all her plans would flash a picture of Rhy, naked, his eyes hungry as he reached for her, and her body would remember his touch and she'd tremble in reaction. She ached for him; why hadn't he come up to the apartment with her last night? Of course they'd both been tired, exhausted and irritable, but still... What a fool she was! The last thing she needed was more of his addictive lovemaking! It would be hard enough now to get over him, to forget again the wild sweetness that had consumed her.

The morning slipped past, and she grimly determined to work through lunch, but her plans were derailed when Chris stopped by her desk, his brown eyes shuttered as he silently lifted her nameplate and studied it, then returned it to her desk without comment. "Can you get away for a little while?" he asked quietly, but even so Sallie caught the undertone in his voice, perhaps because she was so miserable herself that she was sensitive to the suffering of others.

"It's lunchtime, anyway," she said without hesitation, turning off the typewriter and covering it. "Where do you want to go?"

"Will he mind?" Chris asked, and she knew who he meant.

"No," she lied, and gave him a cheeky little grin. "Besides, I'm not asking him."

He didn't speak again until they were out of the building and weaving their way through the hurrying, dodging, sidestepping lunch crowd that filled the sidewalks. He lifted his head and peered at the heat ball of the sun with slitted eyes as he commented, "Are you really married to him? It's not easy to get married that fast unless you detour through Vegas."

"I've been married to him for eight years," she admitted, not meeting the questioning glance that she felt him shoot at her. "And we've been separated for seven of those years."

They walked in silence for a while, then Chris caught her hand and indicated a coffee shop. That was as good as anything and they went inside, where they were shown to a small table along the wall. Sallie wasn't hungry and she chose only fruit juice to drink and a small salad, knowing that the salad wouldn't be eaten. Chris didn't seem very hungry either, for when their food came he merely drank his coffee and stared broodingly at the tuna sandwich on his plate.

"It looks as if you're back together now," he finally said.

Sallie shook her head. "It's what he wants."

"And you don't?"

"He doesn't love me," she said sadly. "I'm just a challenge to him. Like I told you, he just wants to play for a while. It doesn't matter to him that he's destroying my life in the process. He's already wrecked my career, and he swears that he'll blacklist me, keep me from getting another job as a reporter."

Chris swore, something he rarely did, and met Sallie's surprised gaze with gold lights of anger leaping in his dark eyes. "How could he do that to you?" he muttered.

She managed a careless shrug. "He says he's afraid I'll get killed. That he can't stand the thought of me in the middle of a revolution." But how many times had Rhy left her to do just that, leaving her behind in a frenzy of worry?

"Now *that* I can understand," said Chris, giving her a wry smile. "I'll admit to having a few worries about your pretty little carcass myself, and I'm not even married to you."

"But you won't quit for Amy," she reminded him bluntly. "And I won't quit for Rhy—if I have any choice. He's hemming me in, Chris. He's tying me down and smothering me."

"You love him."

"I try not to. I just haven't succeeded very well so far." Then she shook her head. "Forget about me. Is the situation still the same with Amy?"

He tilted his head a little to one side. "I still love her. I still want to marry her. But she still won't marry me unless I quit reporting, and the thought of stifling myself in a nine-to-five job makes me break out in a cold sweat."

"Can you give in? Greg did, for his kids."

"But he didn't for his wife," Chris pointed out. "He had to lose her before he left the field. If she were still alive he'd probably still be out there chasing down a story."

That was true and she sighed, looking away from him. The demands made by children were so much harder to deny than those made by adults because children saw things only in relation to themselves and couldn't comprehend that their parents' needs should be as important as their own. They had no compunction about making their needs clear, demanding that they be taken care of, while adults for some reason drew back, refrained from pushing too hard, knowing that no one owed them anything and therefore they didn't ask. Except she had asked—she had demanded—that Rhy change his job and stay with her, and it had gained her exactly nothing. Rhy had made it plain that her happiness wasn't his responsibility. He had his own life to live. Nor could she offer Chris any hope, any solution, for she could see none for herself. No matter what they did, misery would be the result.

"I'm going to leave," she said aloud, then looked at him in horror, not having meant to announce her intentions.

He caught the look and waved his hand. "Forget it. It won't go any further," he assured her. "I kind of thought you might do that, anyway. You've got the guts to do what you have to do, no matter how it hurts. You're cutting your losses. I just wish I could."

"When you're ready you will. Don't forget, I've had seven years to get used to being without him." She gave him a tiny smile. "I'd even convinced myself that it was all over between us. It didn't take Rhy long to shatter that little fairy tale."

He looked at her as if he wasn't really seeing her, his dark eyes taking on the introspective blankness of someone walling himself up inside. He'd been hurt, just as she had. There was nothing so calculated to batter the self-esteem as to hear a loved one saying, "You have to change," the insidious little phrase that really meant, "I don't love you as you are. You're not good enough." There were deeper hurts, more violent hurts, yet somehow that particular hurt had such a nasty sting. She knew it well now, and she swore that she'd never ask anyone to change ever again. Had Rhy been hurt by her insistence that he change? She tried to picture a confused, hurt Rhy and failed utterly. He had a stainless-steel character that never faltered, never let itself be vulnerable. He'd brushed her clinging arms off like so many cobwebs and went on his way.

"I'll get over her," said Chris quietly, and on his face was the smooth blank look of acceptance. "I guess I'll have to, won't I?"

They walked back to the office in silence, and as they entered the empty elevator Chris punched the button to close the door and held his finger on it, staring fixedly at her.

"Keep in touch," he said softly. "I wish it could've been you, Sal." He curved his hand around her neck and bent to lightly touch his lips to hers and she felt tears sting her eyelids. Yes, why couldn't it have been Chris for her, instead of Rhy?

She couldn't promise that she'd be in touch, though she wanted to. Once she left she couldn't risk doing anything that might give Rhy a clue to where to find her, and anything Chris didn't know he couldn't divulge. She left the elevator with only a long look into his face that said goodbye; then she went back to her desk and tackled the report again with grim determination.

The sense of now or never gave her the concentration she needed and in less than an hour she sent the finished report on to Greg's office. She stood and stretched her tired, cramped muscles and casually got her purse and left the building without speaking to anyone, as if she was merely leaving for an appointment, when in reality she intended never to return. She regretted that she had to leave without telling Greg, but he'd made it painfully clear that his first loyalty was to Rhy, and she knew that he would immediately report her resignation.

Caution made her cash the cashier's check she'd been carrying in her purse and convert most of the money into traveler's checks. Who knew what means Rhy might use to hold her? She had to get out and do it now.

It was almost three-thirty by the time she reached her apartment and it was only instinct, but when she opened the door the hair on the back of her neck lifted. She stared around at the familiar furniture and she knew that something was different. Looking about she saw that several things were missing: her personal awards were gone, her books were gone, her antique clock was missing. Thieves!

Rushing into the bedroom she stared aghast at the emptiness. The closet doors stood open, revealing the lack of contents. Her cosmetic and toiletry items were gone from the bathroom, even her toothbrush. All of her personal items had disappeared! Then she went utterly pale and raced back into the bedroom to stare in horror at the uncluttered surface where her manuscript and typewriter had rested. Even her manuscript had been stolen!

A noise in the doorway made her whirl, ready for battle if the thieves had returned, but it was the landlady who stood there. "I thought I saw you," Mrs. Landis said cheerfully. "I'm so happy for you. You're such a nice girl, and I always wondered when you were going to get married. I'll hate losing you, but I know you're anxious to settle in with that handsome husband of yours."

A cold feeling settled in Sallie's stomach. "Husband?" she echoed weakly.

"He's the first celebrity I've ever met," Mrs. Landis rattled on. "But he was so nice, and he said he'd made arrangements for your furniture to be put in storage by this weekend so I can rent the apartment out again. I thought it was so thoughtful of him to handle it all for you while you were working."

By now Sallie had gotten control of herself, and she managed a smile for Mrs. Landis. "It certainly was," she agreed, her hands clenching into fists by her sides. "Rhy thinks of everything!"

But he hadn't won yet!

Chapter Nine

She was so angry that she was shaking helplessly, unable to decide what to do. She got on a bus and rode aimlessly, wishing violently that she could get her hands around Rhy's throat. He'd literally stolen her clothing, all of her personal possessions. That was bad enough, but she could get along without all that if she had to. The one thing she couldn't leave behind was her manuscript, and she couldn't think of any way to get it back, either. She didn't even know where Rhy lived, and his telephone number wasn't listed.

But she had to find somewhere to spend the night, and at last she left the bus and walked the teeming sidewalks in the steamy hot afternoon sun until weariness prompted her to choose a hotel at random.

She checked in and sat for a long time in a daze, unable to think of any action she could take. Her mind darted about erratically, trying to devise a way of retrieving the manuscript without having to see Rhy again. But to find the book she had to find out where Rhy lived, and to do that she had to talk to him, something that she wanted to avoid.

The theft of her book seemed to have paralyzed her, robbed her of her ability to act. She thought bleakly of simply beginning again, but she knew that it wouldn't be the same; she couldn't remember all of the details of her exact phrasing. She cried for a while, out of anger and despair, and when she finally decided to call Rhy at the office she realized that she'd waited too long; everyone would have gone home.

So there was nothing to do but wait. She showered, lay on the bed and watched television, then drifted to sleep with the set still on, only to waken in the early hours of the morning to the crackle of static.

She was starving because not only hadn't she eaten the lunch she'd chosen, she hadn't had dinner the night before, either, and her empty stomach was the last straw; curling up like a child she wept brokenly. How *dare* he!

But Rhy would dare anything, as she knew to her cost. She drifted back to sleep and when she woke again she had a pounding headache and it was nearly ten a.m. She took another shower and dressed, then breathed deeply several times and sat down by the phone. There was no way out of it. She had to talk to him.

Before her courage deserted her she dialed the office number and asked for Mr. Baines. Of course Amanda answered and Sallie managed a calm good morning before she asked to speak to Rhy.

"Of course, he said to put you through immediately," Amanda replied cheerfully, and Sallie's nerves screamed with tension as she waited for Rhy to come on the line.

"Sallie." His dark, rough-velvet voice in her ear made her jump and bang the receiver against her already aching temple. "Where are you, darling?"

She swallowed and said hoarsely, "I want my book back, Rhy!"

"I said, where are you?"

"The book—" she began again.

"Forget the damned book!" he rasped, and it was all her nerves could stand. She gulped, trying to swallow the sob that tore out of her throat, but it was swiftly followed by another and abruptly she was crying helplessly, clinging to the receiver as if it was a lifeline.

"You—you stole it!" she accused between sobs, her words almost unintelligible. "You knew it was the one thing I couldn't leave without and you stole it! I hate you, do you hear? I hate you! I never want to see you again—"

"Don't cry," he said roughly. "Baby, please don't cry. Tell me where you are and I'll be there as soon as

I can. You can have your book back again, I promise."

"Written on water!" she jeered, wiping her wet cheeks with the back of her hand.

He drew an impatient breath. "Look, you'll have to see me if you want the book back. And since that seems to be the only hold I have on you, I'll use it. Meet me for lunch—"

"No," she broke in, looking down at her wrinkled slacks and top. "I—I'm not dressed."

"Then we'll have lunch at my apartment," he decided briskly. "I'll phone the housekeeper and have a meal prepared, so meet me there at twelve-thirty. We can talk privately there."

"I don't know where you live," she confessed, surrendering to the inevitable. She knew it was an error to see him again; she should just leave the manuscript and forget about it, try to start again, but she couldn't. Whatever the risk, she couldn't leave without it.

He gave her the address and instructions on how to get there, and just before he hung up he asked gently, "Are you all right?"

"I'm fine," she said bleakly, and dropped the receiver onto its cradle.

She got up to brush her hair and stared aghast at her reflection in the mirror. She was pale, hollow eyed, her clothing wrinkled. She couldn't let Rhy see her like this! And she didn't have so much as a tube of lipstick in her purse!

But she did have money, and there were shops on the ground floor of the hotel. Making up her mind, she took the elevator down and hurriedly purchased an attractive white summer dress with a tiny floral design on it and a pair of white high-heeled sandals.

In another shop she bought makeup and perfume; then she dashed back up to her room. Carefully she made up her face and repaired the ravages of tears and worry, then dressed in the dainty cotton dress and brushed her hair out; she didn't have the time to do anything with it so she left it streaming down her back in a rich sable mane.

She took a taxi to Rhy's apartment, too nervous to face the crush of a bus at lunchtime. When she got out at his apartment building she glanced at her watch and saw that she was a few minutes late. She paid the taxi driver and hurried to the elevator and punched the button.

As soon as she rang the doorbell the door swung open and Rhy loomed before her, his dark face expressionless.

"I'm sorry I'm late—" she began, rushing into speech in an effort to disguise her nervousness.

"It doesn't matter," he interrupted, standing aside to let her enter. He'd discarded his jacket and tie and unbuttoned his shirt halfway, revealing the curls of hair on his chest. Her eyes riveted on his virile, masculine flesh and unconsciously she wet her lips with her tongue. Just the sight of him weakened her!

His eyes darkened to charcoal. "You teasing little witch," he muttered, and his long fingers moved to his shirt. He unbuttoned the remaining buttons and pulled the shirt free of his pants and peeled out of it, dropping it to the floor. The sunlight streaming through the wide windows gleamed on his chest and shoulders where a light dew of perspiration moistened his skin and revealed all his rippling muscles.

Sallie stepped back, wanting to escape from the need she felt to touch his warm skin and feel the steelness of muscle underneath, but she made the mistake of raising her eyes to his. The hungry, blatant desire she saw there froze her in her tracks.

"I want you," he whispered, advancing on her. "Now."

"I didn't come here for this," she protested weakly, and made a futile attempt to evade him. His long arms encircled her and pulled her against his half-naked body, and she began to tremble at the erotic power he had over her. The scent of his skin, the warmth, the living vibrancy of him, went to her head and intoxicated her so that she forgot about pushing him away.

He attacked with his mouth, overpowering her with kisses that demanded and devoured, sucking all of her strength away so she couldn't resist when his shaking hands moved over her curves and renewed his intimate knowledge of her. She raised her arms and locked them around his neck and kissed him back, her response burning out of control and fanning his own fires.

She rested plaintively against him when he raised his head to gulp in deep, shaking breaths and the half smile that formed on his mouth before being quickly banished revealed that he was aware of his triumph, of her capitulation. With slow, easy moves, as if he didn't want to startle her, he unzipped her dress and slid it down to puddle around her feet. Sallie simply watched him in silence, her big eyes nearly black with desire. She couldn't resist; she couldn't make any plans. All she could do was feel, feel and respond. She loved him and she was helpless against his love.

But at least her desire was returned. She was dimly aware that he was shaking, trembling in every muscle of his big frame as he lifted her gently into his arms and carried her into his bedroom. He placed her on the bed and lay down beside her, his hands pulling at the bits of clothes that remained to separate skin from skin. He couldn't disguise his need for her, just as she had no defenses against him. Hoarsely he whispered to her, disjointed words and phrases that made her quiver in response and cling to him as she drowned in the tidal wave of sensation he evoked.

When the world had righted itself again she was lying in his arms while he slowly stroked her hair, her back, her arms. "I didn't intend for that to happen," he murmured against her temple. "I'd planned to talk first, eat our lunch together and try to act like two civilized people, but the moment I saw you nothing was important any longer except making love to you."

"That's all you ever wanted from me anyway," she said with simple, weary bitterness.

He gave her a brooding glance. "You think so? That's part of what I wanted to talk about, but first, let's see about lunch."

"Won't it be cold?" she asked, pushing her hair back from her face and sitting up and away from his arms.

"Steaks and salad. The salad is in the fridge, the steaks are ready to grill. And I gave Mrs. Hermann the rest of the day off so we won't be disturbed."

"You have everything planned, don't you?" she commented without any real interest as she began dressing, and he swung his long legs over the side of the bed to stand and watch her lethargic movements.

"What's wrong?" he asked sharply, coming to her and cupping her chin in his hand to look into her pale face. "Are you ill?"

She felt ill, achy and depressed after the soaring passion of his lovemaking, and she was stupidly weak. But she knew that her only ailments were an inability to cope with Rhy and the fact that she hadn't eaten in over twenty-four hours.

"I'm well enough," she dismissed his concern. "Just hungry, I suppose. I haven't eaten since yesterday morning."

"Great," he half snarled. "You need to lose some more weight. You must weigh at least ninety pounds. You need someone to watch you and make certain you eat, you little fool!"

He probably had himself in mind, but she didn't argue with him. In silence she completed dressing and waited until he had dressed also. Then she followed him into the neatly organized kitchen. He refused to let her do anything and made her sit on a stool while he grilled the steaks and set the places on the table in the small dining room.

He opened a bottle of California red wine to drink with the meal and for several minutes they ate in silence. Then Sallie asked without looking up from her salad, "Where is my manuscript?"

"In the study," he replied. "You've got a way with words. It's good reading."

She flung her head back as anger struck her. "You had no right to read it!"

"Didn't I?" he asked dryly. "I thought I had a perfect right to read what you'd been writing all those days when you were supposed to have been working for my magazine. You've been drawing a check every week and not writing a word of the articles assigned to you. If it hadn't suited me to keep you quietly at your desk I'd have fired you weeks ago."

"I'll repay every penny I've drawn since you bought the magazine," she flared. "You still had no right to read it!"

"Stop spitting and scratching at me, you little cat," he said in amusement. "I did read it, and there's nothing you can do about it now. Instead, think constructively. You've got a manuscript with strong possibilities, but it's also got some rough edges, and there's a lot of work that needs to be done on it. You need a place to work on it where you won't be disturbed, and you certainly don't need to worry about paying the rent or buying groceries.''

"Why not?" she muttered. "Thousands of writers worry about those things."

"But you've never had to," he pointed out. "For your entire life you've had financial security, and it's something you're used to. You won't have a paycheck coming in now, because you're off the payroll as of yesterday, and it'll worry you when your savings begin shrinking. It takes time to write a book and get it on the market. You'll run out of money before then."

"I'm not a helpless baby and I'm not afraid of work," she replied.

"I know that, but why worry about any of that when you can live here, work on your book without interruptions and keep your savings?"

She sighed, feeling trapped. On the surface it was a logical suggestion, but she knew that the proposal was only a way of getting her back under his thumb where he thought she belonged. If she had any sense she would leave at the first opportunity, even if she had to sacrifice the manuscript, but she'd already passed up one such opportunity and she painfully admitted to herself that it was too late for her to gain her freedom. She was caught again in her own stupid, helpless love for Rhy, knowing that her love wasn't returned except in the lowest form—physical desire. He desired her, and for that reason he wanted her around now, but what would happen when he tired of her again? Would he simply walk out as he had before? Knowing that she was leaving herself wide open for another broken heart she stared into her salad and said expressionlessly, "All right."

He drew in a quick breath. "Just like that? No arguments, no conditions? Not even any questions?"

"I'm not interested in the answers," she replied, shrugging. "I'm tired of fighting you, and I want to finish my book. Other than that, I don't care."

"You're great for a man's ego," he muttered under his breath.

"You trampled all over mine," she snapped in reply. "Don't expect kid gloves from me. You've got what you wanted, me out of a job and living with you, but don't ask for blind adoration because I'm fresh out."

"I never asked for it anyway," he rasped. "And for the record, I'm not trying to chain you down. It was that particular job that I objected to, for reasons you know. All I'm asking from you is time for us to be together, to try to work things out. If we can't stand to live together for six months I'll consider a divorce, but the least we can do is give it a try."

"And if it doesn't work out we'll get a divorce?" she asked cautiously, wanting to be certain.

"Then we'll talk about it."

Glancing at his implacable face she saw that he wasn't going to give her a promise of a divorce so she gave in once more. "All right, six months. But I'm going to be working on my book, not cooking for you and washing your clothes and cleaning this place. If you're looking for a little homemaker you're going to be disappointed.''

"In case you haven't noticed, I'm a wealthy man," he said sarcastically. "I don't expect my wife to do laundry.''

She lifted her head and stared at him. "What are you getting out of this, Rhy? Other than a sleeping companion, I mean, and you can have that anytime you please without going to all this trouble.''

His lids shadowed his gray eyes and he murmured huskily, "Isn't that enough? I want you. Let's just leave it at that.''

To Sallie's surprise the arrangement worked rather well and they quickly fell into a routine. Rhy would get up every morning and prepare his own breakfast, then wake her with a kiss when he was ready to leave. She would linger over her own breakfast, then spend the rest of the morning in the study, working. Mrs. Hermann turned out to be a plump, gray-haired model of efficiency, and she took care of the apartment just as she had before, making Sallie lunch, cooking the evening meal and leaving just before Rhy arrived home.

Sallie would serve dinner herself, and while they were eating Rhy would tell her about how things were going with the magazine, what had happened that day, ask questions about how her book was progressing. She found herself remarkably at ease with him now, though their relationship never quite achieved true companionship. She sensed that they were both holding something of themselves back, but perhaps that was to be expected when two people with such strong wills tried to live together. There was always the thought that good manners should prevail or the frail fabric of their marriage would be torn beyond repair.

As the days turned into weeks and the stack of pages in the study kept growing she welcomed Rhy's advice and experience. Her own writing style was direct and uncomplicated, but Rhy had the knack of stripping an idea down to the bare bones. It became their custom after dinner for him to read what she'd written that day and give her his opinion. If he didn't like something he said so, but he always made it plain that he thought her overall effort was good. Sometimes she threw out entire sections and began anew, all on the basis of Rhy's criticisms, but at other times she stubbornly clung to her own words as she felt that they better conveyed her own meaning.

Her best work seemed to be done in the evenings when Rhy sat in the study with her, reading articles and paperwork he'd brought home with him or doing his preliminary research on the documentary he was scheduled to film within three months. He seemed content, all traces of the restlessness she remembered gone, as if he had indeed burned out his need for adventure. In an odd way she was also content; the mental stimulation she received from creating a book was more than enough to occupy her imagination.

They worked together in harmony and relative silence, broken only by the ringing of the telephone when Greg called, as he often did, and their own occasional comments to each other.

Then, when it was growing late, Sallie would cover the typewriter and leave Rhy still working while she bathed and prepared for bed. Sometimes he would work for an hour or more after she was in bed, sometimes he followed her closely to the shower, but always—always—he would get in bed with her and take her in his arms and the restrained civility of their manner would explode in hungry, almost savage lovemaking. She had thought his passion would wane as he grew used to having her around again, but his desire remained at a high pitch. Occasionally when they worked together she would watch his absorbed face, fascinated that he could look so calm now yet turn into a wild sensualist if she were to put her arms around him and kiss him. The thought teased at her brain until she would ache to do just that, to see if she could divert his thoughts from his work, but over the years she had developed a deep respect for a person's work and she didn't disturb him.

Only two incidents broke the surface harmony of those first weeks. The first occurred early one evening as she was clearing away the dinner dishes and putting them in the dishwasher. Rhy was already in the study, reading what she'd written that day, so when the phone rang she answered it on the kitchen extension.

"Is Rhy there? Could I speak to him, please?" asked a cool feminine voice and Sallie recognized it instantly.

"Certainly, Coral, I'll get him to the phone," she replied, and placed the receiver on the cabinet top while she went to the study.

He looked up as she entered. "Who was that?" he asked absently, looking down at the pages in his hand.

"It's Coral. She wants to speak with you," Sallie replied in amazingly level tones, and returned to the kitchen to finish her chores. The temptation to listen in on the kitchen extension made her pause for a second, but only a second, then she firmly replaced the extension.

She tried to tell herself that it was nothing but jealousy eating at her insides. Coral had enough self-possession that if she wanted to see Rhy she would have no scruples about calling him at home. Were they still seeing each other? Rhy never mentioned where he went for lunch—or with whom—and about once a week he was late getting home in the evening. As engrossed as she was in the progress of her book she hadn't really noticed or thought anything of it, and she also knew that deadlines had to be met and things could happen that would make a long day necessary.

But Coral was so breathtakingly beautiful! How could any man not be flattered that such a lovely woman obviously adored him?

She couldn't stand it if Rhy was still seeing her, Sallie knew. For a while she had convinced herself that it didn't matter to her if Rhy had other women because she was over him, but now she knew differently. She loved him, and all her defenses had been shattered. He had won a complete victory, if he only knew it, but somehow she had kept herself from admitting aloud that she loved him. He never mentioned love, so neither did she.

When she didn't return to the study Rhy came in search of her and found her standing in the kitchen with her hands clenched.

"Aren't you coming—" he began, then cut his words off when he saw her taut face.

"I can't stop you from seeing her," Sallie said harshly, her eyes black with pain and fury. "But don't you dare let her call you here! I won't put up with that!"

His face darkened and his jaw tightened with temper. It was as if the weeks of politeness had never been. At the first sign of hostility their tempers broke free like wild horses too long held under control. "Hadn't you better get your facts straight before you make wild accusations?" Rhy snarled, coming forward to glower down at her. "You should've listened on the extension if you're so interested in my activities! As it happens, Coral asked me to have lunch with her tomorrow, and I refused."

"Don't deny yourself on my account!" she hurled rashly.

His lips twisted in a travesty of a smile. "Oddly enough, I've been doing just that," he ground out between his teeth. "But now, with your permission, I'll show you just what I *have* been denying myself!"

Too late she moved, trying to avoid his hands as they darted out to catch her, but he swung her up in his arms and strode rapidly to the bedroom. Furiously Sallie twisted and kicked but the difference in their sizes and strength left her helpless against his powerful body. He dropped her on the bed and followed her down, capturing her mouth with his and kissing her with such angry demand that her struggles turned abruptly into compliance. They made love wildly, their pent-up frustrations erupting in the force of their loving.

Afterward he held her clamped to his side while, with his free hand, he stroked over her nude body. "I'm not seeing Coral," he muttered into her hair. "Or any other woman. The way I make love to you at night should assure you of that," he concluded wryly.

"It made me see red when she called," Sallie admitted, turning her head to brush her lips across his sweaty shoulder.

She could feel the tremor that ran through his body as her lips touched him and his arm tightened about her. "You were jealous," he accused, self-satisfaction evident in his tone. She gasped in a return of anger and tried to wiggle away from him, only to be hauled back against him for another whirlwind possession.

The second incident was her fault. One morning she decided to go shopping, the first time she'd done so since Rhy had moved her in with him. She needed several little things, and she passed the morning pleasantly, then decided to stop by and see her old friends at the magazine, maybe eat lunch with Rhy if he wasn't busy.

First she poked her nose into the large room where she'd worked and was greeted loudly and cheerfully. Brom was off on assignment, and for a moment she felt a twinge of envy, then the exuberant welcome of the others made her forget that she was no longer a free-flying bird. After several minutes she excused herself and went up for a few minutes with Greg. She wasn't certain that she'd ever forgive him completely for switching over to Rhy's side, even though she was now living with her husband in relative harmony, but Greg was an old friend and he was dedicated to his job. She didn't want any coolness between them.

After a restrained greeting she and Greg rapidly regained their former easy mood. They parted with Greg's grinning comment that having a full-time husband must be good for her, she looked contented.

Like a cow, Sallie thought to herself in amusement as she went up to Rhy's office. She was still smiling when she stepped off the elevator and literally ran into Chris.

"You're back!" he exclaimed in instant delight, holding her at arm's length and looking her over. "You're blooming, darling!"

Sallie's eyes widened in dismay as she realized that she hadn't let Chris know that she was still in town. Greg knew, of course, but Greg wasn't exactly talkative about personal details. "I've never been gone," she admitted ruefully, smiling up into his dark eyes. "Rhy caught me."

Chris's eyebrows rose. "You don't look as if you're wasting away," he drawled mildly. "Maybe the situation isn't as bad as you thought it'd be?"

"Maybe," she said laughing. "Greg just told me that I look *contented!* I can't decide if I'm insulted or not."

"Are you really happy, honey?" he asked in a gentle tone, and all of his joking was gone.

"I'm happy in a realistic way," she replied thoughtfully. "I don't expect heaven anymore, and I won't be destroyed when what I have ends."

"Are you so sure that it will?"

"I don't know. We just take every day as it comes. We manage to get along now, but who can say that it'll always be like that? What about you? Did you and Amy...?" She stopped, looking into the level, accepting brown eyes, and she knew that he was alone.

"It didn't work." He shrugged, taking her hand and leading her to the window at the end of the hallway, away from the elevator doors. "She's married to that other guy now, she won't even talk to me on the phone."

"I'm sorry," she murmured. "She got married so soon. I thought she wasn't supposed to marry him until later this year?"

"She's pregnant," Chris said rawly, and for a moment his face twisted with his inner pain, then he drew a deep breath and stared at Sallie with wry self-mockery. "I think it's my baby. Well, maybe it's the other guy's, I don't know, but I know that it could be mine, too. I'm not even sure Amy knows. I don't care. I'd marry her in a minute if she'd have me, but she said I'm too 'unstable' to be a good father."

"You'd marry her even knowing that she'd slept with another man while she was going out with you?" Sallie asked in amazement. That was love, love that accepted anything.

He shrugged. "I don't know what she did, but it wouldn't make any difference to me. I love her and I'd take her any way I could get her. If she called me now I'd go to her, and to hell with her husband." He said it in a calm, flat tone, then he shook his head. "Don't look so worried," he advised, a smile coming to his face. "I'm all right, honey, I'm not falling apart."

"But I care about you," she protested weakly.

"And I care about you." He grinned down at her and suddenly lifted her in his arms, swinging her around giddily, laughing as she protested. "I've missed you like mad," he told her, his brown eyes turning impish. "I don't trust anyone else to give me advice on my love life—"

"Take your damned hands off my wife."

The toneless words were dropped like stones and Sallie struggled out of Chris's grip to whirl and find Rhy standing just outside his office door, his eyes narrowed to slits. Automatically she looked at his hands. They weren't curled into fists but were slightly cupped, his long fingers tense through his arms, his stance, relaxed and loose. Those hands could strike without warning, and Rhy looked murderous. She moved forward, casually putting herself between Rhy and Chris, but Rhy moved to the side and another clear path to Chris. As he moved Amanda came out of the office and stopped in her tracks at the sight of Rhy's bloodless face.

Chris didn't seem disturbed; he remained relaxed, his mouth curling into a wry smile. "Easy there," he drawled in his slow, humorous tone. "I'm not after your woman. I've got enough woman trouble of my own without taking on someone else's."

By then Sallie had reached Rhy, and she put her hand on his arm, feeling the rigid muscles there. "It's true," she told him, smiling like mad in an effort to hide the fear that had her heart thudding. "He's madly in love with a woman who wants him to settle down and stop dashing off to other countries at the drop of a hat, and he likes to tell me all about it. Does the plot sound familiar?"

"All right," Rhy uttered, his lips barely moving. His face was still frozen in white rage, but he growled at Amanda, "Go on to lunch. Everything's okay."

After Amanda and Chris had left she and Rhy stood in the hallway staring silently at each other. Gradually he relaxed and said tiredly, "Let's get out of this hallway. The office is private."

She nodded and preceded him into his office, and no sooner was the door closed behind them than he caught her in his arms, holding her to him so tightly that her ribs protested in pain.

"I've never been out with him," she managed to reassure him as she gasped for breath.

"I believe you," he whispered raggedly, his lips brushing across her temple, her cheek, the corner of her eye. "I just couldn't bear to see you in his arms. You're mine, and I don't want any other man touching you."

Her heart pounding, Sallie lifted her arms about his neck and clung to him. She was giddy with hope. The violence of his reaction couldn't be simple possessiveness; his emotions had to be involved to some extent for him to be shaking like this, his hands almost punishing as he touched her. But she couldn't be certain, and she held back the most reassuring phrase of all that trembled on her tongue: I love you. She couldn't say it to him yet, but she had begun to hope.

"Hey, I came to see if you want to have lunch with me," she finally said gaily, lifting her head from its resting place on his shoulder.

"That's not what I want," he growled, his eyes straying suggestively to the sofa, "but I'll settle for lunch."

"I'm afraid we caused a scandal," she teased as she walked beside him to the elevator. "It'll be all over the building before the end of the day."

He shrugged negligently. "I don't care. Let it be a warning to any of your other pals who might want to hug you. I'm a throwback, a territorial animal, and I don't allow any encroachment into that territory."

At once she felt an icy shaft of pain in her heart. Was that all she was to him, a part of his territory? Thank heavens she'd kept silent a moment ago instead of blurting out her feelings for him! She was a fool to look for any deeper feelings from him; he didn't have any, and she'd always known that. He *was* a throwback, his instincts swift and primitive. He saw to the satisfaction of his needs and didn't waste time on anything as foolish as love.

Chapter Ten

The sense of accomplishment she felt as she stared at the last page of the manuscript surpassed anything she'd experienced as a reporter. It was finished! No longer was it a figment of her imagination. It existed; it had an identity. She knew there was still a lot of work to be done on it, rereading, correcting, rewriting, but now it was, for all intents and purposes, complete. Her hand reached for the telephone; she wanted to call Rhy and share this moment with him, but a wave of dizziness made her fall back weakly in the chair.

The dizziness was only momentary, but when it had passed she remained as she was, the impulse to call Rhy having faded. That was the fourth spell this week.... Of course. Why hadn't she realized? But perhaps she'd known all along and hadn't allowed the thought to surface until now. The book had claimed all of her attention, all of her energy, and she had pushed herself to complete it. But as soon as it was finished her subconscious had released the knowledge of her pregnancy.

Glancing at the desk calendar she decided that it had been the first night in Sakarya. "When else would it have been?" she murmured to herself. That was the first time in seven years Rhy had touched her, and she had immediately become pregnant. She gave a smile of self-mockery, then the smile became softer and she drew the calendar to her to count the weeks. Her baby would be due around the beginning of spring, and she thought that was a wonderful sign, a new beginning.

This baby would live, she knew. It was more than a new life, it was a strengthening of the fabric of her marriage, another bond between her and Rhy. He would make a wonderful father now, much better than he would have been years before. He would be delighted with his baby.

Then she frowned slightly. Filming on the documentary was scheduled to begin next month, and Rhy had planned on taking her with him. He might change his mind if he knew she was pregnant. So she wouldn't tell him until after they returned! She wasn't about to let him leave without her; it would be a rerun of their early days, and she wasn't sure enough of either him or herself yet to endure a long separation.

She realized that she had a lot to do before then; first and foremost she needed to see a doctor and make certain everything was normal and that traveling wouldn't hurt the baby, and begin taking the recommended vitamins. She should also buy new clothing, because by the time the filming was done she would probably have outgrown her present wardrobe. She pictured herself round and waddling and grinned. Rhy had missed most of her first pregnancy, but this time she would insist that he help her to do all of the little things she'd had to manage by herself before, like getting out of bed.

Of all the nights for Rhy to be late, she thought, he had to pick this one. He called at five and told her wearily that it would probably be eight or later when he made it home. "Eat without me, baby," he instructed. "But keep something hot for me. I don't think I can face a sandwich."

Swallowing her disappointment, she agreed, then suggested jokingly, "Do you need any help? I'm an old hand at meeting deadlines."

"You don't know how tempting that offer is." He sighed. "But work on the book instead, and I'll be home as soon as I can."

"I finished the book today," she informed him, her fingers tightening around the receiver. "So I'm taking a break." She had wanted to tell him when he first walked in the door, but she couldn't wait that long.

"You did what? Oh, hell," he said in disgust and Sallie's mouth trembled in hurt surprise. Then he continued, and she brightened again. "I should be taking you out to celebrate instead of working late. But I'll be home as soon as possible, then we'll do some private celebrating, if you understand my meaning."

"I thought you were tired." She laughed and his low chuckle sounded in her ear.

"I am tired, but I'm not dead," he replied huskily. "See you in a few hours."

Smiling, she replaced the receiver. After eating her solitary dinner she took a shower and settled down in the study to begin rereading the book, scribbling changes and corrections in the margins as she went. The work was absorbing, so much so that when she heard Rhy's key she was surprised at how swiftly the time had passed. She shoved the manuscript aside and jumped to her feet, then had to cling to the back of a chair for a moment when dizziness assailed her. Slowly. She must remember to move slowly.

Rhy entered the study, his tired face breaking into a grin as he surveyed her attire, a transparent dark blue nightgown and matching wrap. He tossed his jacket aside and tugged his loosened tie completely off, throwing it on top of his jacket. He began unbuttoning his shirt as he came to her. "Now I understand the charm of coming home to a negligee-clad wife," he commented as he slid his arms around her and pulled her up on tiptoe for his kiss. "It's like a shot of adrenalin."

"Don't become too fond of the practice," she warned. "I just took my bath early because I had nothing else to do. Are you very hungry?"

"Yes," he growled. "Are you going to make me wait?"

"You know I meant for food!" Laughing at him, she crossed to the door. "Wash up while I set the table. I've kept things warm."

"Don't bother with the dining room," he called. "The kitchen is fine with me, and a lot handier."

She did as he instructed and set his plate in the kitchen. He joined her there and while he ate they discussed the book. Rhy had already talked to an agent that he knew, and he wanted to hand the book over before they left for Europe.

"But it isn't ready," Sallie protested. "I've already begun making corrections for retyping."

"I want her to read it now," Rhy insisted. "It's a rough draft. She won't expect it to be word perfect right now."

"She?" Sallie asked, her ears pricking up.

"Yes, she," he mocked, his gray eyes glinting. "She's a bone-thin bulldozer by the name of Barbara Hopewell, and she's twenty years older than I am, so you can draw in your claws."

Sallie glared at him. She had the feeling that he'd purposely tricked her into revealing her jealousy and she didn't want him to gain too much of an advantage on her.

"Why are you in such a hurry?" she demanded.

"I don't want you worrying about the book while we're in Europe. Hire a typist, do whatever you have to, but I want the book out of the way before we leave."

Because she was feeling resentful over his gibe about jealousy she propped her elbows on the table and gibed back at him. "Has the thought occurred to you that now that the book's finished I'll be bored sitting around here all day? I need to be looking for a job, not jaunting around Europe."

If she'd wanted to rile him she succeeded beyond her wildest expectations. He turned pale; then two hectic spots of temper appeared on his high cheekbones. Slamming his fork down on the table he reached across and grasped her wrist, hauling her to her feet as he stood up himself. "You never miss a chance to twist the knife, do you?" he muttered hoarsely. "Sometimes I want to break your neck!" Then he jerked her against him and brutally took her lips, not allowing her a chance to speak even if she could have thought of anything to say, and with their mouths still fused he slipped one arm behind her knees and lifted her easily, her slight weight nothing to his powerful arms.

Sallie had to cling to him; the swift movement as he jerked her to her feet had made her head swim alarmingly and she felt as if she might faint. Neither could she understand why he had reacted so violently, or what he meant about twisting the knife. Confused, all she knew was that she'd made him angry when she hadn't really meant to, and she offered him the only comfort she could, the response of her lips and body. He accepted the offer hungrily; the pressure of his mouth changing from hurtful to persuasive, and he carried her to the bedroom.

Afterward she lay curled drowsily against him, wrapped in the security of his own special male scent and the warmth of his nearness while he lazily stroked her abdomen and pressed kisses along the curve of her shoulder.

"Did I hurt you?" he murmured, referring to his urgent lovemaking, and Sallie whispered a denial. "That's good," he replied huskily. "I wouldn't want to..." He paused, then after a moment continued. "Don't you think it's time you told me about the baby?"

Sallie sat bolt upright in the bed and turned to stare at him with huge eyes. "How did you know?" she demanded in astonishment, her voice rising. "I only realized it myself today!"

He blinked as if she'd jolted him in return; then he tipped his dark head back against the pillow and roared with laughter, tugging her down to lie against his chest. "I should've guessed," he chuckled, his hand smoothing her long hair away from her face. "You were so wrapped up in that book you didn't even know what day it was. I knew, darling, because I'm not a complete ignoramus and I can count. I thought you were deliberately keeping me in the dark because you didn't want me to have the satisfaction of knowing you're pregnant."

"Gee, you must think I'm a lovely character," she muttered crossly and, turning her head, she sank her teeth playfully, but firmly, into his shoulder. He yelped in pain and instantly she kissed the wound, but she told him defiantly, "You deserved that."

"Out of consideration for your delicate condition I'll let you get away with that," he mocked, tilting her face up for a kiss that lingered.

"Actually," Sallie confessed a moment later, "I wasn't going to tell you just yet."

His head snapped around, and he cupped her chin in his palm, forcing her to look at him. "Why?" he growled.

"Because I want to go to Europe with you," she stated simply. "I was afraid you'd make me stay here if you knew I'm pregnant."

"Not a chance. I wasn't with you before, but I'm planning on being with you every day of this pregnancy—with your permission, Mrs. Baines, I'll even be with you when our baby is born."

Her heart stopped, then lurched into overtime. Too overcome to speak, Sallie turned her face into his shoulder and held him with desperate hands. Despite everything he had ever said—and all the things he had never said—she began to hope that Rhy really did care for her. "Rhy—oh, Rhy!" she whispered in a choked voice.

Misunderstanding the cause of her emotion he gathered her close to him and stroked her head. "Don't worry," he murmured into her hair. "This baby will be all right, I promise you. We'll get the best obstetrician in the state. We'll have a houseful of kids, you wait and see.''

Clutching him to her Sallie thought that she'd be satisfied with only this one, if it lived. That, and Rhy's love, would make her life complete.

Caught up in a whirlwind of activity preparing for the trip to Europe, which included readying not only her own clothing but Rhy's as well, as he was working late more and more often in an effort to tie up all loose ends before they left, and hammering the book into its final shape, Sallie hardly had a moment to think during the next few weeks. The doctor had assured her that she was in perfect shape, though she could stand to gain a few pounds, and the baby was developing normally. He was also in favor of the trip to Europe so long as she remembered to eat properly.

She had never been happier. Four months ago she had thought that Rhy meant nothing to her, and all she wanted was to be free of his restricting influence. She still fumed sometimes at the high-handed methods he'd used to restore her to her position as his wife, but for the most part she was glad that he didn't know how to take no for an answer. She was more deeply in love with him now than she'd ever been as an insecure teenager, for she'd grown in character in those years away from him. Her feelings were stronger, her thoughts and emotions more mature. Now he acted as if he never wanted her out of his sight, and he seemed so proud of the child she carried that she sometimes thought he was going to hang a sign around her neck announcing her expectant state.

Disaster struck without warning a week before they were due to leave for Europe. It was one of those picture-perfect autumn days when the sunshine was warm and the sky was deep blue, yet the air carried the unmistakable fragrance of approaching winter. Sallie made one last shopping trip, determined that this would be *it*, and took her purchases home. She felt marvelous, and her eyes sparkled and her skin glowed; she was smiling as she put away the articles of clothing she had bought.

Her senses had always been acute, but she still had no warning of what was to come when the doorbell rang and she called out to Mrs. Hermann, "I'll get it. I'm right here!"

She pulled the door open, smiling warmly, but the smile faltered as she recognized Coral Williams. The model looked beautiful, as always, but there was a haunted expression on the exquisite face that made Sallie wonder uneasily if Rhy had been wrong, if Coral was suffering because he'd stopped seeing her.

"Hello," she greeted the other woman. "Will you come in? Is there anything I can do for you?"

"Thank you," Coral replied almost inaudibly, walking past Sallie and standing uncertainly in the foyer. "I . . . is Rhy here? I tried to phone him, but his secretary said he's out of the office and I thought he might perhaps . . ." Her voice trailed off and pity welled up in Sallie's throat. She knew all too well how it felt to suffer from the lack of Rhy's love, and she was at a loss as to what to do. She sympathized with Coral, but she wasn't about to hand over Rhy to the other woman, even if Rhy was willing.

"No, he's not here," Sallie replied. "He's often out of his office now. He's very busy preparing for our trip to Europe."

"Europe!" Coral turned very white, only her expertly applied makeup supplying any color to her cheeks. She was unnaturally pale anyway and the severely tailored black dress she wore only pointed up the hollows of her cheeks and her generally fragile appearance.

"He's filming a documentary," explained Sallie. "We expect to be gone about three months."

"He—he can't!" Coral burst out, clenching her fists.

A sudden chill ran up Sallie's spine and unconsciously she squared her shoulders as if in anticipation of a blow. "What is it you want with Rhy?" she challenged directly.

Coral stiffened too, staring down at Sallie from her superior height. "I'm sorry, but it's private."

"I don't accept that. If it concerns Rhy it concerns me. He *is* my husband, you know," she ended sarcastically.

Coral winced as if Salllie'd scored a hit, then recovered herself to say scornfully, "Some husband! Do you really think he spared a thought for you when you were separated? The old adage of 'out of sight, out of mind' was never more true than with Rhy! He was out with a different woman every night, until he met me.''

Sallie shuddered with the sudden violent desire to punch Coral right in that perfect mouth. The woman was only saying what she'd always thought herself, though privately she wanted very much to believe Rhy's assertions that his relationships with other women had been platonic. Certainly she couldn't fault his behavior since she'd been living with him again. A woman couldn't ask for a more attentive husband.

''I know all about your relationship with Rhy,'' she declared solidly. ''He told me everything when he asked me to come back to him.''

''Oh, did he?'' Coral asked wildly, her voice rising in shrill laughter. ''I doubt that. Surely some details are still private!''

Abruptly Sallie had had enough and she moved to open the door again so Coral could leave. ''I'm sorry,'' she said firmly. ''I'm asking you to leave. Rhy's my husband and I love him and I don't care what his past is. I'm sorry for you because you lost him, but facts are facts and you might as well face up to them. He won't come back to you.''

''What makes you so certain of that?'' Coral yelled, losing all control, her face twisting with fury. ''When he hears what I've got to tell him he'll come back to me, all right! He'll leave you without even a consoling pat on the head!''

For a moment the woman's certainty caused Sallie to waver; then she thought of the child in her womb, and she knew that Rhy would never leave her now. "I don't think so," she said softly, playing her ace. "I'm pregnant. Our baby will be born in March. I don't think any of your charms can equal that in Rhy's view."

Coral reeled backward as if she might faint, and Sallie watched her in alarm, but the woman recovered herself and burst into peal after peal of mocking, hysterical laughter, holding her arms across her middle as if she found Sallie's announcement hilarious. "Priceless!" she gasped when she had enough breath for words. "I wish Rhy could be here. This lacks only his presence to be the hit comedy of the year!"

"I don't know what you're talking about," Sallie broke in stiffly, "but I think you'd better go." The amused, malicious glitter in Coral's eyes made her uncomfortable, and she wanted only for the woman to leave so she could be alone again and recapture her mood of confident serenity.

"Don't be so sure of yourself!" Coral flared, her hatred plain on her face. "You managed to pique his interest by acting as if you wanted nothing to do with him, but surely you know by now that he's incapable of staying faithful to any one woman! I understand him. Some men are just like that, and I love him despite his weakness for other women. I'm willing to allow him his little affairs so long as he comes back to me, whereas you'll drive him mad with boredom within a year. And don't think a baby will make any difference to him!''

Beyond Coral, Sallie saw Mrs. Hermann hovering in the doorway, her round face frowning with worry as she listened to Coral's abusive tirade. Instinctively disliking having a witness to the nasty scene Coral was creating Sallie jerked the door open and snapped, "Get out!"

"Oh, I'm glad to go!" Coral smirked. "But don't think you've got everything your way! Women like you make me sick, always acting so sure of yourselves and sticking your noses in where they don't belong, thinking some man will admire you! That's why Rhy pulled you off of foreign assignments, he said you were making a fool of yourself trying to act as tough as any man. And now you think you're something special just because you're pregnant! That's nothing so special. Rhy's good at getting women pregnant!''

Despite herself Sallie reeled in shock, not quite certain she understood what Coral was saying. The sight of her suddenly pale face seemed to give Coral some satisfaction because she smiled again and spat out, "That's right! The baby you're carrying isn't the only child Rhy has fathered! I'm pregnant, too, and it's Rhy's baby. Two months pregnant, honey, so tell me what that means about your perfect marriage! I told you, he always comes back to me!''

Having delivered her blow Coral stalked out with her head held at a queenly altitude. Unable to completely take in what the woman had said Sallie closed the door with quiet composure and stared across the room at Mrs. Hermann, who had pressed a hand over her mouth in shock.

"Mrs. Baines," Mrs Hermann gasped, her voice rich with sympathy. "Oh, Mrs. Baines!"

It was then that Sallie understood just exactly what Coral's words had meant. She was pregnant, and it was Rhy's baby. Two months pregnant, she had said. So Rhy had not only lied about his relationship with Coral, he'd continued it after his reconciliation with Sallie. In dazed horror she thought again of all the nights when Rhy had supposedly been working late. She'd never thought to call him at the office to check up on him. She would have been insulted if Rhy had checked up on her, so she'd accorded him the same respect and he'd abused it.

Numbly she went past Mrs. Hermann into the bedroom, Rhy's bedroom, where she'd spent so many happy nights in his arms. She stared at the bed and knew she couldn't bear to sleep there again.

Without thinking about it she jerked down the suitcases from the top of the closet and began filling them helter-skelter with the clothing she'd bought to take to Europe. She had money and she had a place to go; there was no reason for her to stay here another minute.

She paused briefly when she thought of the manuscript, but it was safely in the hands of Barbara Hopewell, and she would get in touch with her later. Later...when she could bear to think again, when the pain had subsided from the screaming agony that was tearing her apart now.

When she carried the suitcases out into the hallway she found Mrs. Hermann there, hovering, wringing her hands in agitation. "Mrs. Baines, please don't leave like this! Try to talk things out—men will be men, you know. I'm sure there's an explanation."

"There probably is," Sallie agreed tiredly. "Rhy's very good with explanations. But I just don't want to hear it right now. I'm leaving. I'm going somewhere quiet and peaceful where I can have my baby, and I don't want to think about my husband and his mistresses."

"But where will you be? What shall I tell Mr. Baines?" the housekeeper wailed.

"Tell him?" Sallie stopped and thought a minute, unable to think of any message that could adequately express her state of mind. "Tell him . . . tell him what happened. I don't know where I'm going, but I know that I don't think I ever want to see him again." Then she walked out the door.

Chapter Eleven

The days passed slowly, dripping out of existence. Like a salmon returning to the place of its birth to spawn and die she had returned to her own origins, the little upstate town where she'd grown up, where she'd met Rhy and married him. Her parents' house was empty and neglected and many of the old neighbors had died or moved on and she didn't know any of the children who played now in the quiet streets. But it was still home, and she moved back into the small house and tidied it up, refurnished it with the minimum of furniture for her needs. Then she waited for time to work its magic healing process.

At first she was unnaturally calm, numbed by her sense of loss and betrayal. She'd just gotten used to living with him, and now she was alone again with the solitary nights pressing down on her like an invisible weight. She didn't try to think about it or straighten it out in her mind; there was no use in driving herself mad with if onlys and might have beens. She had to accept it, just as she would have to if he'd died.

In a sense that was what had happened. She'd lost her husband as irrevocably as if he had died. She was as alone, as empty. He was in Europe now, half a world away, and he might as well have been on another planet.

Then she realized that she was neither alone nor empty. His baby moved inside her one day and she stood with her hands pressed over the gentle fluttering, overcome by the feeling of awe that a living creature was being nurtured inside her body. Rhy's baby, a part of him. No matter if she never saw his face again she would always have him near. That thought was both painful and comforting, a threat and a promise.

The numbness wore off abruptly. She woke in the dark, silent hours before dawn one morning, and her entire body ached with the pain of her loss. For the first time she cried, weeping with her face pressed into the pillow, and she thought about it endlessly, trying to understand the hows and whys of his behavior. Was it her fault? Was it something about her that challenged Rhy to subdue her, then forced him to lose interest once she was captured? Or was it Rhy's own nature, as Coral had charged, an inability to be faithful to one woman?

Yet that denoted a certain weakness of character, and that didn't describe Rhy. A lot of adjectives could be used to describe him—arrogant, hot-tempered, stubborn—but weakness in any respect wasn't one of them. She would also have sworn on his professional integrity, and she felt that integrity was not an isolated thing in a person, restricted to only one field; integrity spread out, showing itself in every aspect of a person's behavior.

So how could she explain his infidelity? She couldn't, and the question tore at her. She forced herself to eat only because of the baby, but even so she grew pale and thinner. Sometimes she woke up in the middle of the night to find her pillow wet, and she wanted Rhy beside her so badly that it was impossible to get back to sleep. At times like that she wondered why she'd run off, like a fool, and left the field clear for Coral. Why hadn't she stayed? Why hadn't she put up a fight for him? He'd hurt her, he'd been unfaithful, but she still loved him and surely it couldn't hurt any more if she'd stayed with him? At least then she'd have had the comfort of his presence; they could have shared the miracle of the growing child she carried. During those dark predawn hours she sometimes determined to pack her clothes first thing in the morning and fly to Europe to join Rhy, but always, when the morning came, she would remember Coral and the baby that she carried. Rhy might not want her to join him. Coral might be with him. Coral was more glamorous anyway, more suited for a life in the limelight with Rhy.

It wasn't in her nature to be indecisive, but for the second time in her life she'd lost her bearings, and both times had been because of Rhy. The first time she had eventually found her feet and pursued a goal, but now she was unable to plan anything more complicated than the basic needs of living. She ate, she bathed, she slept, she did what had to be done. She had read enough to know that part of her lethargy was due to being pregnant, yet that wasn't excuse enough to explain her total lack of interest in anything beyond the next moment.

As the late fall days passed and winter drew closer she became aware that Christmas was near. Somehow every Christmas since the death of her parents had been spent alone, and this one would be no different. But next year, she promised herself, gazing at a brightly decorated tree as she made her weekly trip to the nearest grocery store, she would have a real Christmas. The baby would be about nine months old, bright eyed and inquisitive about everything in its world. She would decorate a tree and pile gifts beneath it that would fascinate a crawling baby.

It was a vague plan, but it was the first plan she'd made since leaving Rhy. For the baby's sake she had to pull herself out of the doldrums. She had a book in the works; she needed to contact the agent and see about publication and perhaps start work on another book. She had to have some means of taking care of the baby or the first thing she knew Rhy would be demanding custody of his child. Fiercely she determined that she'd never allow that to happen. Rhy had another child; she only had this one and she'd never let it go!

Two weeks before Christmas she finally made a firm decision and dialed Barbara Hopewell's office with her former briskness. When Barbara came on the line Sallie identified herself, and before the other woman could say anything she asked if any progress had been made in locating a publisher.

"Mrs. Baines!" Barbara gasped. "Where are you? Mr. Baines has been going mad, trying to complete filming in Europe and flying back here every free moment he has in an effort to trace you! Are you in town?"

"No," Sallie replied. She didn't want to hear about Rhy or how hard he'd been looking for her. Oddly enough, she'd expected that he would make an effort to find her if only because of the child she carried. "And where I am doesn't matter. I only want to discuss the book, if you don't mind. Has a publisher been found?"

"But..." Then Barbara changed her mind, and she answered in an abrupt tone, "Yes, we have a publisher who is extremely interested. I really need to schedule a meeting with you, Mrs. Baines, to go over the details of the contract. May I make an appointment?"

"I don't want to return to New York," Sallie said, her throat constricting at the thought.

"Then I'll be glad to meet you wherever you want. Just set the time and tell me the location."

Sallie hesitated, unwilling to divulge her hiding place, yet equally unwilling to leave it for a meeting at any other location. Then she quickly added up the dates and realized that Rhy would still be filming in Europe for another month. Barbara had said that he flew back as often as he could, but she knew that schedule, and it was a tightly packed one. The odds were that he would be unable to leave on a moment's notice even if Barbara did happen to be in touch with him and let slip that she'd talked to Sallie.

"All right," she agreed reluctantly and gave Barbara her address. They agreed on a time that Thursday for Barbara to come to the house.

That was only two days away and Sallie felt even more confident that Rhy wouldn't find out her hiding place. When she saw Barbara on Thursday she would get her promise not to tell Rhy; she hadn't wanted to discuss the matter over the phone, knowing that anyone in Barbara's office could listen in on an extension.

She couldn't sleep that night; she was too anxious that she had made a mistake in revealing her bolt hole to relax. Somehow she had the feeling that Rhy was one step ahead of her, as usual. Lying in her bed, tense and unable to close her eyes, she imagined all sorts of what ifs: What if Rhy had been in New York even then? What if Rhy had even been in Barbara's office and was on his way upstate now? What if she got up in the morning to find him on her doorstep? What would she say to him? What was there to say?

Tears seeped from beneath her lids as she squeezed them slightly shut in an effort to banish the picture she suddenly had of Rhy's dark, lean face. Pain pierced her sharply and she turned on her side to weep, hugging the pillow to her face in an effort to stifle the sobs. "I love him," she moaned aloud. That hadn't changed, and every day apart from him was an eternity.

Abruptly, desolate in her loneliness, she admitted to herself that she wanted to go back to him. She wanted his strength, his physical presence, even if she couldn't have his love. She wanted him there to hold her hand while she gave birth to their child and she wanted to have other children. The thought of Coral and that other baby tore at her insides, but gradually she was realizing that her love, her need, for Rhy was stronger than her anger. She had to accept him as he was if she wanted to live with him.

She dozed eventually, toward dawn, and woke only a few hours later to the steady, dreary sound of cold rain pouring down. The sky was gray, the streets stark and cheerless. Snow had not yet arrived and given everything its winter-wonderland effect, but the trees were denuded of leaves and the bare branches rattled against each other like bones of a skeleton. There was nothing to get up for but she did, and managed to occupy herself by trying to work out a sketchy outline for another book. This one would be more difficult, she knew, for the first one had been partially rooted in her own experiences. This one would have to be totally from her imagination.

By midafternoon the rain had stopped but the temperature had dropped, and when she turned on the television she learned that the rain was supposed to begin again later that night, then turn to sleet and snow before morning. Sallie made a wry face at the weatherman on the screen. It was possible that bad road conditions would keep Barbara from making their appointment and she felt horribly disappointed. Her interest in the world around her was returning and she wanted to get on with the business of living.

After an hour of pacing around, boredom overcame her and she felt stifled in the small house. It was cold outside, and damp, but she felt that a brisk walk would clear the cobwebs from her mind and perhaps relax her enough so she could sleep that night. Not only that, she told herself righteously, but the doctor had wanted her to take some form of exercise every day. A walk was just the thing.

She wrapped herself up warmly, pulling on knee-high boots and shoving her hair up under a dark fur hat that covered her ears. After buttoning her heavy coat up and wrapping a muffler about her throat she set off briskly, shivering at first in the cold air, but gradually movement warmed her and she began to enjoy having the streets to herself. It was almost sundown and the dreary sky made it that much darker. The water dripping from the trees onto the sidewalk and street was the only sound except for the clicking of her boots, and she shivered again but not from the cold this time. Why was she walking like an idiot when she could be back safe and snug in her warm house?

*And why was she running from Rhy when all she
wanted was to be back in his arms?*

Stupid, she mentally berated herself as she headed
for home. Stupid, stupid, stupid! And spineless on top
of that! She would be the biggest fool alive if she left
the field clear for Coral! When this weather cleared up
and she could travel safely she'd leave for Europe on
the first plane out, and if she found Coral with Rhy
she'd tear out all of that gorgeous blond hair. Rhy
would not get off completely free, she promised herself, the light of battle sparkling in her eyes. She had
a lot to say to him, but she meant to keep him! After
all, hadn't these past seven years taught her that he
was the only man for her?

Retracing her steps faster now, she turned the corner and came in sight of her house. She was so caught
up in her plans that at first she didn't see the taxi in
front of her house; it wasn't until a tall man who
moved with the litheness of a panther ducked down to
pay the driver that her gaze was drawn to the cab. She
stopped in her tracks and the breath stopped in her
chest as she stared at the proudly held dark head, bare
despite the dripping trees. The taxi pulled away with a
flash of red taillights and the man set a single flight
bag on the wet sidewalk and stared at the house as if
mesmerized by the sight of it. No lights were on and it
could have been empty, she realized, except for the
curtains that covered the windows. Was that what he
was thinking? she wondered with sudden pain. That
it was empty after all?

"Rhy," she whispered and began walking again. The sound of her boots drew his attention and his head turned swiftly, like that of a wild animal sensing danger. He froze for a moment, then began walking toward her with a purposeful stride. Just like him, she thought, trying not to smile. There was no self-doubt in that man. Even when he was wrong he was confident.

But when he was close, when he stopped with only three feet separating them, she had to bite her lip to keep from crying out with pain. His lean face bore the marks of suffering; there were harsh shadows under his steely eyes and lines that hadn't been there before. He was tired of course, and the grayness of exhaustion enhanced the grimness of his expression. He'd lost weight; the skin was pulled taut over the high, proud cheekbones.

He shoved his hands deep into the pockets of his overcoat and stared at her, his bleak gaze roving over her small, delicate face and her rounded form beneath her coat. Sallie quivered with wanting to throw herself into his arms, but he hadn't opened them to her, and she was suddenly afraid that he didn't want her. But why was he here?

"She lied," he said tonelessly, his voice even harsher than before and almost beyond sound. His lips were barely moving as he seemed to force out his next words. "I'm dying without you, Sallie. Please come back to me."

Incredulous joy rocketed through her veins, and she closed her eyes for a moment in an effort to control herself. When she opened them again he was still staring down at her with a desperate plea in his gray eyes, his lips pressed grimly together as if he expected the worst. "I was planning on it," she told him, her voice tremulous with joy. "I'd just now decided that as soon as the weather cleared I was taking a plane to Europe."

A shudder quaked visibly through his body; then he pulled his hands out of his pockets and reached for her at the same time that she stepped forward. Hard arms enfolded her in a tight, damp embrace, and she put her arms around his neck and clung desperately, tears of happiness running down her face. He caught her mouth with his and held it, kissing her deeply and re-assuring both of them that they were together again; then he lifted her completely off the ground, turning round and round on the sidewalk in a slow circle as they kissed.

At some point it began to rain again; they were both soaked by the time Sallie glanced up at the pouring skies and laughed. "What fools we are!" she ex-claimed. "Why don't we go inside instead of standing out in the rain?"

"And you don't need to catch a chill," he growled, putting her on her feet and leaning down to lift his flight bag. "Let's get dried off, then we can talk."

He insisted that she take a hot shower while he changed into dry clothing, and when she came out of the bath she found that he'd made coffee; two steam-ing cups were already on the table.

"Oh, that's good." She sighed as she sipped the hot liquid and it completed the warming job that the shower had started.

Rhy sank into a chair at the table and rubbed a hand over the back of his neck. "I need this to keep me awake," he said wearily.

Sallie looked at him, seeing his exhaustion etched into every line of his face, and her heart clenched painfully. "I'm sorry," she said softly.

He made a gesture with his hand, waving aside his weariness, and silence stretched between them. It was as if they were afraid to begin, afraid to say anything personal, and Sallie stared into her coffee cup.

"Chris is gone," said Rhy abruptly, not looking at her.

Her head jerked up. "Gone?" she echoed.

"He quit. Downey told me—hell, I don't know how long ago it was. Everything's a blur. But he quit, said he was moving on to another city."

For a moment Sallie had hoped that Chris and his Amy had gotten together, that he'd quit his job to settle down, but she knew that it just hadn't happened for Chris. A shaft of pain pierced her as she thought of how close she'd come to losing Rhy, and she quickly took another sip of coffee. She blurted, "I suppose Barbara called you?"

"Immediately," he acknowledged. "I owe her a lot to make up for that favor. I completely wrecked the shooting schedule to get on the first flight to New York. Everyone thinks I've gone berserk anyway, flying back and forth cross the Atlantic whenever we had a break. It drove me crazy," he admitted grimly. "Not knowing where you were, if you were all right, knowing that you believed what that vicious little tramp told you."

"Mrs. Hermann told you what she said?" Sallie asked, wanting to know if Coral's story had been related correctly. Wild hope was bubbling in her; he'd said that Coral had lied, and he certainly wasn't acting like a man who was guilty of anything.

"Word for word, with tears pouring down her face like a waterfall," Rhy growled. He reached out abruptly and took Sallie's free hand, clasping it firmly in his long fingers. "She lied," he told her again, his husky voice taut with strain. "If you've ever believed anything, believe that. Coral may be pregnant, but I swear I'm not the father. I've never made love to her, though she tried hard enough to instigate an affair."

The words jolted Sallie. His voice had an undeniable ring of truth to it, but still she squeaked incredulously, *"Never?"*

A flush darkened his cheekbones. "That's right. I think I was a challenge to her ego. She just couldn't believe that I wasn't interested in sleeping with her even when I told her I was married and that I'd never been as attracted to any other woman as I was to my wife," he said, watching her steadily. Sallie blushed under his regard, and his hand tightened on hers. "I think she hated you because of that," he continued, his eyes never leaving her face. "I turned her down in favor of you, and she tried her best to tear us apart, to hurt you. Maybe she didn't plan on doing what she did, if you want to give her the benefit of the doubt. If she truly is pregnant she probably wanted me to give her the money for an abortion. A pregnancy is poison to a model, and I can't see Coral as a doting mother."

Sallie sucked in her breath. "Rhy, would you have?"

"No," he growled. "And I could've killed her when Mrs. Hermann told me what she'd done."

"But... surely Coral has the money herself...?"

"Don't you believe it," he muttered. "She likes the high life too well to save anything and she loses heavily in Atlantic City and Vegas. She's not a good gambler," he finished starkly.

"But why did you go out with her at all if you weren't interested in her?" Sallie asked. That was the biggest flaw in Rhy's story. He and Coral had been constant companions, and she wasn't fool enough to think things hadn't progressed beyond hand-holding.

"Because I liked her," he replied abruptly. "Don't ask me for proof of my faithfulness, Sallie, because I haven't got any. I can only tell you that Coral wasn't my mistress, even before I found you again."

"Take it on trust?" she queried, her voice going tight.

"Exactly," he said in a hard voice. "Just as I have to take it on trust that you haven't been involved with any other man. You have no proof, either."

Sallie scowled down at the tablecloth and traced a pattern on it with the hand he wasn't holding. "I've never been interested in any other men," she admitted with ill-grace, hating having to reveal that secret to him. "I've never even bothered to date."

"And for eight years you've been the only woman I could see," he replied in a strained voice, releasing her hand and getting up to stride restlessly around the small kitchen. "I felt like a fool. I couldn't understand why a timid little rabbit like you were then had gotten under my skin like that. I wouldn't have put up with one scene over my work from any other woman, but I kept coming back to you, hoping you'd grow up and understand that I *needed* my work. You said you were hooked on excitement, on danger, and that's exactly the way I was. A danger junkie.

"I never meant to leave you permanently," he said jerkily. "I just wanted to teach you a lesson. I wanted you to beg me to come back to you. But you didn't. You picked up and carried on as if you didn't need me at all. You even sent my support checks back to me. I buried myself in work. I swore I'd forget about you, too, and sometimes I almost did. I enjoyed the company of other women, but whenever things began getting involved . . . I just couldn't. It made me furious, but I'd remember how it had been with us, and I didn't want second best."

Sallie stared at him, thunderstruck, and he glared at her as if she'd done something terrible. "I made a lot of money," he said with constrained violence. "A lot of money. I bought some stocks and they went out of sight and I ended up a rich man. There was no longer any need to put myself on the line to get a story and getting shot at had lost whatever perverted thrill it had held for me, anyway. I wanted to sleep in the same bed every night, and finally I admitted to myself that if there was going to be a woman in that bed it had to be you. I bought the magazine and began trying to trace you, but you'd left here years before, and no one had any idea where you were."

"You tried to find me?" she asked, her eyes going wide with wonder. So Rhy hadn't simply forgotten about her for those years! "And this time? You've been trying to find me this time, too?"

"It seems like trying to find you has become a habit." He tried to make a joke, but his face was too tightly drawn to express any humor. "I didn't even think of hunting for you here. I've been checking with newspapers in all the major cities on the thought that you were likely to get a job as a reporter. You threw it in my face so often that you were bored without a job that I thought you'd go right back to work."

"I thought I'd be bored," she admitted, "but I wasn't. I had the book to work on, but most of all, you were there."

His face lightened curiously. "You sure put up a good fight, lady," he said wryly, and he gave her a wolfish grin that held no humor.

"I didn't have a chance," she denied. "Having me working for your magazine like I did gave you all the aces."

"Don't you believe it," he said roughly. "I caught a glimpse of a long braid swinging against a slim little bottom, and it was like I'd been kicked in the gut. Without even seeing your face I wanted you. I thought it was a vicious joke on me to find a woman I wanted just when I'd begun the search for my wife, but the few glimpses I had of you made me determined to have you. Then I ran into you in the hallway and recognized you. The dainty little elf with that bewitching braid was my own wife, changed almost beyond recognition except for those big eyes, and you made it plain that you weren't interested in anything about me. I'd spent eight years with the feel of you branded on my senses until I couldn't even see another woman, and you didn't care!''

"Of course I cared!" she interrupted, standing up to face him. She was trembling with strain, but she couldn't let him think that he meant nothing to her. "But I didn't want you to hurt me again, Rhy! It nearly killed me when you left the first time, and I didn't think I could stand it again. I tried to protect myself from you. I even convinced myself that I was completely over you. But it didn't work," she finished in a small voice, staring down at the tiled floor.

He drew a deep, shaking breath. "We're two of a kind," he said roughly. "We're as wary and independent as wild animals, the both of us. We try to protect ourselves at all costs, and it's going to be hard to change. But I *have* changed, Sallie. I've grown up. I need you more than I need excitement. It's hard to say," he muttered. "It's hard to deliberately leave yourself open to hurt. Love makes a person vulnerable, and it takes a lot of trust to admit that you love someone. Why else do people try so hard to hide a love that they know isn't returned? I love you. You can tear me to pieces or you can send me so high I lose myself. Trust has to start somewhere, Sarah, and I'm willing to make the first move. I love you.''

Hearing him call her Sarah swept away all the long years of loneliness and pain, and she raised a face that was pale and streaked with slowly falling tears. ''I love you, too,'' she said softly, making the words a litany of devotion. ''I've always loved you. I ran away because I was hurt. I was insecure and didn't feel that you loved me, and Coral tore me apart with her vile insinuations. But today I decided that I loved you too much to just let you go, hand you over to her without a fight. I was coming after you, Rhy Baines, and I was going to make a believer out of you!''

''Hey,'' he said just as softly, opening his arms and holding them open for her. ''Go ahead. Make me believe it, darling!''

Sallie dived into his arms and felt them enclose her tightly. She couldn't stop the tears that wet his neck, and he tried to comfort her, gently kissing the moisture from her cheeks and eyes.

They had been apart for too long. His kisses became hungry and his hands roamed over her gently swelling body, and Sallie cried out wordlessly as desire flamed through her. He lifted her and carried her to the bedroom, the same bedroom where eight years before he'd carried her as an innocent bride and initiated her into the intoxicating sensuality of his lovemaking. It was the same now as it had been then; he was gentle and passionate, and she responded to him with all her reserve finally gone. When the fire of their desire had been sated she lay drowsily amid the tangled covers of the bed. His dark tousled head was pressed into her soft shoulder and his lips sleepily nuzzled the swell of her breast. His lean fingers stroked the slight swell his child made and he murmured against her flesh. "Was it all right? There's no harm in making love?"

"None," she assured him, lacing her fingers tenderly in the thick hair that curled onto his neck. She couldn't get enough of touching him; she was content to lie there with him resting heavily against her, worn-out from traveling and their loving.

He was already half-asleep but he muttered, "I don't want to tie you down. I just want you to fly back to me every night."

"Loving you doesn't tie me down," she answered, kissing his forehead, which was all she could reach. And it didn't. She was surprised. Where had all her fears for her independence gone? Then she knew that what she'd really feared had been being hurt again. Rhy's love would give her a springboard to soar to heights she'd never reached before. She was free as she'd never been before, free because she was secure. He didn't hold her down; he added his strength to hers.

"You've got talent," he whispered. "Real talent. Use it, darling. I'll help you in any way I can. I don't want to clip your wings. I fell in love with you all over again when I found you, you'd grown up, too, and become a woman who drove me mad with your nearness and wild with frustration when we were apart."

Sallie smiled in the darkness. It looked as if all those crash courses so long ago had finally paid off.

He went to sleep on her shoulder, and she slept, too, content and secure in his love. For the first time she felt that their need for each other was something permanent. She had always felt the tug of the bond that held her to him, but until now she hadn't known that he was equally bound to her. That was why there had been no divorce, why he hadn't even made an effort to obtain one. They belonged to each other and they always would.

* * * * *

Take 3 of "The Best of the Best™" Novels FREE

Plus get a FREE surprise gift!

Special Limited-time Offer

Mail to The Best of the Best™

3010 Walden Avenue
P.O. Box 1867
Buffalo, N.Y. 14269-1867

YES! Please send me 3 free novels and my free surprise gift. Then send me 3 of "The Best of the Best™" novels each month. I'll receive the best books by the world's hottest romance authors. Bill me at the low price of $3.74 each plus 25¢ delivery and applicable sales tax, if any.* That's the complete price and—compared to the cover prices of $4.50 each—quite a bargain! I understand that accepting the books and gift places me under no obligation ever to buy any books. I can always return a shipment and cancel at any time. Even if I never buy another book from Harlequin, the 3 free books and the surprise gift are mine to keep forever.

183 BPA ANV9

Name	(PLEASE PRINT)	
Address	Apt. No.	
City	State	Zip

This offer is limited to one order per household and not valid to current subscribers.
*Terms and prices are subject to change without notice. Sales tax applicable in N.Y.
 All orders subject to approval.

UBOB-94   ©1990 Harlequin Enterprises Limited

Silhouette Books
is proud to present
our best authors, their best books...
and the best in your reading pleasure!

Throughout 1994, look for exciting books
by these top names in contemporary
romance:

JULIE ELLIS
The Only Sin in May

FERN MICHAELS
Golden Lasso in May

DIANA PALMER
The Tender Stranger in June

ELIZABETH LOWELL
Fire and Rain in June

LINDA HOWARD
Sarah's Child in July

*When it comes to passion,
we wrote the book.*

BOBQ2

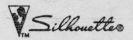